Also by Jamie Russell

SkyWake Invasion
SkyWake Battlefield

JAMIE RUSSELL

WALKER
BOOKS

This is a work of fiction. Names, characters, places and incidents are either the product of the author's imagination or, if real, used fictitiously. All statements, activities, stunts, descriptions, information and material of any other kind contained herein are included for entertainment purposes only and should not be relied on for accuracy or replicated as they may result in injury.

First published 2023 by Walker Books Ltd
87 Vauxhall Walk, London SE11 5HJ

2 4 6 8 10 9 7 5 3 1

Text © 2023 Jamie Russell
Cover illustration © 2023 James Fraser

The right of Jamie Russell to be identified as author of this work has been asserted in accordance with the Copyright, Designs and Patents Act 1988

This book has been typeset in Berkeley Oldstyle

Printed and bound by CPI Group (UK) Ltd, Croydon CR0 4YY

All rights reserved. No part of this book may be reproduced, transmitted or stored in an information retrieval system in any form or by any means, graphic, electronic or mechanical, including photocopying, taping and recording, without prior written permission from the publisher.

British Library Cataloguing in Publication Data:
a catalogue record for this book is available from the British Library

ISBN 978-1-4063-9753-6

www.walker.co.uk

For Mum, with thanks for all the books

THE STORY SO FAR...

Casey Henderson (gamertag: **CASEY_FLOW**) has discovered that her favourite video game, *SkyWake*, isn't just a game. It's actually a secret training tool created by an evil alien race, the Arcturians (aka the Red Eyes), who are using it to train teen gamers to fight in a war on a distant alien planet.

Invited to a gaming tournament in a London shopping centre to find the UK's best *SkyWake* players, Casey met her online teammates – **FISH_HEAD_04**, **SPOCK5_BR@IN**, **XxxEL1TESN1P3RxxX** and **CH33ZEMUNK3Y** – in real life for the first time.

When the Red Eyes invaded the tournament, they abducted hundreds of players, including Casey's little brother, Pete, and egotistical YouTube streamer Xander Kane. Casey and her teammates were the only ones able to fight back using the skills they'd learned from the game. During the battle, Casey discovered the power of "flow: that state of mind when you're totally in the zone.

After failing to stop the Red Eyes on Earth, Casey and the rest of the gamers were taken into deep space and forced to fight on the planet Hosin. Here they found the Red Eyes locked in an endless battle with their mortal enemies, the tentacled, telepathic Bactu (aka the Squids).

As Casey and her teammates tried to escape from the battlefield, the Squids reached out to her. They explained that the Red Eyes were searching for an ancient Bactu artefact called the psionic array, a tool that could be used to take over the galaxy. In return for Casey's help, the Squids showed her how to develop telepathic powers. Casey used these new abilities to fight the Red Eyes, including her nemesis, Scratch.

When Pete and Xander discovered that the legendary psionic array was actually hidden on Earth, they decided to join forces with the Red Eyes in an attempt to get themselves home safely. Torn between heading back to Earth to prevent a Red Eye invasion and saving Hosin from a planet-killing bomb, Casey and her team decided to stay behind to protect the Squids.

With the bomb successfully stopped, Casey and her friends headed home in pursuit of the Red Eyes.

But, after a malfunction on their ship's hyperdrive, they arrive home *four years* later than planned! In this time, the Red Eyes have overrun the planet and, with Pete and Xander's help, found the psionic array. They're now ready to activate it.

Armed with everything they've learned from their adventure on Hosin, can Casey and her friends stop the Red Eyes before it's too late?

0

YOU CAN'T SELL DAD ON EBAY

Three months after Casey's dad died, her mum decided it was time to clear out his belongings. She started early one Saturday morning in a flurry of activity. Clothes were removed from wardrobes, papers were sorted into piles marked *Keep* and *Shred*, and the rest of his possessions were laid out on the double bed in her parents' room.

Casey watched from the doorway as her mum hugged each jumper and checked shirt, inhaling what little scent of her husband remained on them. Then, one by one, she put the clothes into black bin bags. It was the bags Casey objected to the most. It seemed wrong. Disrespectful, almost.

"Why is she doing this now?" Casey's little brother Pete asked as they made breakfast together. He was four years younger than Casey, small for his age, and had a habit of asking her annoying questions as if she was his own personal Alexa.

"Because she thinks it's the right time," Casey explained, passing him a bowl of cornflakes. "Don't make a fuss. It's hard enough on her already."

"It's hard on all of us," Pete muttered, hitting the TV remote. He ate in silence, his eyes fixed on the screen, the spoon passing mechanically from bowl to mouth and back again. Casey poured her dry cereal back into the box. She didn't feel hungry.

An hour later, Mum came downstairs with six bin bags full of clothes and two more packed with paper destined for the shredder. Casey could tell that she'd been crying.

"Who should we donate the clothes to?" Mum asked them, trying to sound upbeat.

"Dad always liked animals," Pete said, muting the TV. "Maybe we can give them to the RSPCA."

Mum nodded, satisfied. She started assembling flat-packed cardboard boxes one by one, sealing their undersides with brown packing tape. The roll screeched as she stretched it out and cut it with her teeth. "The next thing we need to decide is what to do with all the video games," she said, half to herself.

Casey and Pete looked at one another uncertainly.

"What do you mean?" Casey asked.

"All those games and console things in your dad's study. There are hundreds of them."

Casey's breath caught in her throat. "You can't give those away! That's Dad's collection. He spent years building it."

"Don't be silly. We're not giving it away. We're *selling* it."

"What?" Pete cried in outrage. "No!"

Mum bit another piece of packing tape off the roll and shrugged. "We could do with the money."

Casey felt sick. Her dad's collection of retro video games was something she and Pete both loved. He'd started building it before they were born, piecing it together cartridge by cartridge, disc by disc. Some of the games were still in their original cellophane, never opened or played because they were so valuable. Others had been imported from Japan, their colourful boxes rare and exotic. There were consoles and computers, too. Ataris, Spectrums, Commodores, Nintendos, Segas, PlayStations, all kinds of kit and hardware, with the cables looped and tied and laid out in drawers. Dad, a soldier in the Royal Engineers, had been a neat freak.

For Casey and Pete, the study had been the video game equivalent of a sweetshop. Dad had been strict – no one was ever allowed in unsupervised –

but whenever he was at home on a Saturday morning, he'd show them some ancient video game like *Manic Miner*, *Donkey Kong*, *Street Fighter* or *Halo*. While they played, he'd talk to them about the game's design and mechanics and explain what made it special. They were the best kinds of lessons.

Mum's voice interrupted Casey's thoughts. "There's also that *Space Invaders* machine in the garage," she went on, assembling the last of the packing boxes. "Someone's going to have to take it away. Bloody great big thing. Maybe we can sell it on eBay…"

"You can't!" Casey cried.

Mum put down the packing tape and turned to face her. "Casey, I know this is hard. But I have to."

"You've never liked gaming," Casey complained. "You always used to say it was a waste of time."

Mum's brow furrowed and she let out a sigh that was deep and sad. Casey instantly regretted her words. She knew how much her mum had suffered since news had come of their dad's death in Afghanistan. He'd died a hero, defusing a car bomb outside a school in Kabul, and he'd been awarded a posthumous medal for bravery. But the medal was no comfort to any of them. They'd spent the last few months wandering around in their own private bubbles of grief.

"I didn't want to worry you about this," Mum said,

taking her daughter's hand. "But we need money. My shifts at the hospital are being reduced and there are debts and bills to pay. Even with your dad's pension I can't make ends meet on my own. If I don't do something soon, we're going to fall behind on the mortgage. You understand what that means, right?"

Casey bit her lip and nodded.

The grim expression clouding over Pete's face told her he did too.

"How much do you think the collection's worth?" Mum asked.

"A lot," Pete chipped in. "Probably thousands."

"*Thousands?* Really?" Mum looked at Casey for confirmation, her eyes wide as dinner plates.

Casey shrugged, feeling conflicted. She didn't want her dad's collection reduced to a price. It was about more than money to him. It was his passion. But if they were at risk of losing the house, maybe they had no choice. Pete stepped in.

"There's a factory-sealed early copy of *Luigi's Mansion* for the GameCube," he told their mum breathlessly. "That must be worth over a thousand pounds alone. Plus, there's an unopened *Mega Man V* Game Boy cartridge and a Hong Kong import of *Super Mario Bros. 2*. That's well rare. Lots of others, too. We'd get loads of money for the whole collection."

"We'll need someone to come and value it first," Casey pointed out.

"Like one of those guys from the second-hand gaming shop?" Pete suggested.

"No," Casey said. "It needs to be someone independent. Not the person you want to buy it, otherwise they'll just give you a low-ball figure." She looked over at her mum hoping she'd understand. Dad had always been great at making deals.

"Where would I find an expert like that?" Mum asked.

"Dad had a card for someone in his office, a guy he used to buy things from. A retro games dealer. He might help us. I can find it, but there's one condition."

"Is there now?" Mum said and arched her eyebrows, amused by the firmness in Casey's voice. "And what condition is that?"

"The *Space Invaders* machine stays," Casey said. "We're not selling it."

"I'm not sure I can agree to that…" Mum began.

"Dad bought it for a couple of hundred quid off that guy in the old games arcade. I was with him. It's half-broken, anyway."

Mum shook her head. "It's so big and ugly."

"I know, but I want to keep it."

Pete rolled his eyes. "It's not even a good game," he

complained. "We should keep something decent like Dad's console collection. *Space Invaders* is stupid. You just move and shoot, and it's the same thing over and over."

Casey put her hands on her hips and waited until her brother was finished. Then she looked at her mum. Now it was her turn to arch her eyebrows questioningly.

"OK," Mum said, with a sigh of exasperation. "It can stay. But you have to help me pack up the rest of the collection and find me the name of that dealer." She headed back upstairs to continue sorting their dad's belongings.

Pete looked at his sister, sullen. "Why do you even like that game?"

"It's the original arcade classic. It's about heroism – one person making a difference and saving the whole world."

"One person can't make a difference," Pete said, his voice bitter. "Just look at what happened to Dad." He pushed past her and headed upstairs after their mum.

Casey wanted to call after him and tell him he was wrong, but she knew he wouldn't listen to her. He never did.

1

THIS PLACE LOOKS LIKE A BOMB HIT IT

Lord Admiral Nelson lay face down in the fountain. The water, green with algae, lapped against his body. The enormous granite column on which he had once stood, proudly overlooking London, had been smashed to smithereens. Huge chunks of it lay all around. The famous black lions at the base of Nelson's Column ignored the mess, staring into the distance in disdain as if it was nothing to do with them.

Casey and her teammates had spent the night hiding in the abandoned Tube tunnels beneath the city, cautiously emerging as dawn broke. They had hoped to find some semblance of the Earth they remembered, but the strange new world they had landed in the night before had not gone away. They stumbled through the empty streets in the early morning sunlight before coming to a stop in the ruins of Trafalgar Square.

The London landmark, normally teeming with commuters and tourists, had been devastated by some battle – it wasn't clear how long ago. It wasn't just Nelson's Column that had been destroyed. The roads were blocked by the wreckage of several black cabs and double-decker buses, their chassis twisted and charred by some unknown force. A rusting Challenger tank sat at the top of Whitehall in the middle of the intersection. Weeds had sprung up between its tracks and a flock of pigeons perched on its gun barrel.

"Whatever happened here, it looks like we totally missed it," Casey said, taking in the scene of destruction. Her voice startled the birds, sending them into the sky in a panicked flap of wings.

Fish tentatively patted the side of the tank as if to prove to himself that it was real. "I bet we put up a proper fight," he said. "We must have thrown everything at them. Fighter jets. Artillery. Nukes. I reckon we gave them hell."

The rest of the gamers stood in silence, trying to process it all. A few days ago, they'd come to London to play in a *SkyWake* tournament designed to find the best players in the world. Casey had met the boys from her online team, the Ghost Reapers, in real life for the first time. Then she'd watched in horror as the Red Eyes had abducted other gamers from the tournament to fight in a war halfway across the galaxy. It certainly hadn't been your average Saturday, that was for sure.

After an attempted rescue mission to another planet and an encounter with the Red Eyes' mortal enemies, the Squids, Casey and her friends had finally made it back home ... but they were too late to save the day. From their perspective the trip through hyperspace had only taken a few seconds. Their spaceship's onboard computer told a different story, though. Delayed in hyperspace by a navigation system malfunction, they'd lost four years of time in the blink of an eye. In their absence the Red Eyes had taken over Earth. Nothing, Casey realized, would ever be the same again.

"*Veni, vidi, vici,*" Brain whispered to himself. He took off his thick spectacles and breathed on them, before gently wiping them on his T-shirt. One lens was cracked so badly it resembled a spiderweb.

"Come again?" asked Elite.

"It's Latin. Something Julius Caesar said: *I came, I saw, I conquered.*"

Elite pursed his lips. "Not the time to be smart, bruv." Then the wannabe rapper grinned. "But I reckon I can get a sick rhyme out of it. *They came, they saw, they totally conquered. Till the Reapers came back and it all went bonkers.*"

"That barely even scans," Brain complained. "You

really are the worst rapper ever."

"We don't have time for bickering," Cheeze cut in. He manoeuvred his hoverchair over the rubble that littered the intersection. Its anti-gravity unit handled the ruined streets much better than his old wheelchair would have done. "Come on, let's try up here."

The group left Trafalgar Square and headed along Whitehall, the heart of the British civil service. The streets were empty and the anonymous government buildings were badly damaged. Downing Street was little more than a crater, the whole block flattened. Casey wondered if the Prime Minister had survived. She'd never liked him much, but she didn't think she wanted him dead.

The devastation continued at the Houses of Parliament. The ancient Gothic building lay in ruins. Big Ben had fared the worst. The famous clock tower had been destroyed and pieces of its internal mechanism – the springs, cogs and giant black hands that had once told the time – lay scattered here and there on the ground. Rubbish, blown by the wind, piled up around the debris.

"Why hasn't anyone cleaned up?" Fish asked.

"Because the Red Eyes don't care," Brain told him. "They're not here to occupy the Earth. They've just come to take what they need."

"The array?"

"Exactly! As soon as they get it, they'll be done with this place. Why bother looking after it?"

As her teammates stared at the damage, Casey's attention was drawn to movement across Parliament Square. People! At last!

A huge throng was slowly gathering outside Westminster Abbey. Casey stared at their faces. They looked thin and sallow, and their cheeks were sunken with hunger. Weirdly, they were all frantically tapping their mobile phone screens, seemingly oblivious to everyone around them.

"What's that all about?" she wondered aloud.

"Maybe they're playing *Pokémon Go*," Fish suggested, following her gaze. "It's really addictive. Did I ever tell you how I fell down a manhole once? Almost broke my neck, but I found a super rare Snorlax and…"

Casey ignored him, moving closer to the growing crowd. Although she was relieved to see some sign of life on the deserted streets, she was disconcerted by how odd it all seemed. A man in a dirty raincoat brushed past them.

"Excuse me, what's going on?" Casey asked, grabbing his arm. The passer-by looked up from his phone momentarily, surprised at being accosted. His eyes were painfully bloodshot.

"I can't talk," he hissed. "I still don't have enough points for food rations and my kids are sick with hunger." He continued tapping his phone as he spoke. He seemed to be playing some kind of game. Coloured blocks fell from the top of the screen, and he swiped left and right with his finger to sort them. A score kept track of his progress. He cursed as he misplaced a red block.

"What's the game?" Casey asked, letting go of his arm.

"*Blocka*, of course," the man replied in an exasperated tone as if he was being asked if water was wet.

"Doesn't look as fun as *Pokémon Go*," Fish muttered. Then, remembering how long it had been since he'd last eaten, he added: "What kind of food do you get?"

"Please," the man said impatiently. "I don't have time for this. Let me concentrate." He walked away, his eyes locked on the screen, finger swiping left and right.

There was a baritone rumble behind them, and two enormous vehicles rolled into view. The first was an olive-green military truck. As it came to a stop, two young soldiers dressed in black uniforms and bright red berets unzipped its canvas-covered rear to reveal stacks of boxes. The crowd surged forward hungrily.

The second vehicle was a Rhino, an Arcturian troop transport, like the ones Casey had seen on Hosin. Its black metal contours and enormous wheels looked strange and futuristic on the streets of London. Four Red Eye aliens climbed out of it, plasma rifles in their hands. A fifth, stationed on the roof-mounted turret, swung his enormous rail gun towards the civilians. The crowd fell silent, cowed with fear.

"Who are those guys?" Fish asked, staring at the soldiers in their black uniforms as they stood on the truck's tailgate. "They look like Nazis."

"They're Red Caps," said a woman holding a wriggling toddler. "They do the Arcturians' dirty work for them. Collaborators." She spat the last word out. The toddler started to whimper.

"Form an orderly queue!" the first soldier yelled. "Have your phones out ready to be scanned. Let's see how many points you've earned! Remember: no points, no food!"

The announcement made the hungry civilians push forward. Casey watched as phone screens were scanned and food packages were thrown from the back of the truck into the hands of the waiting crowd. In the crush, the woman with the toddler dropped her package. A bright orange paste resembling baby food leaked out. She scrabbled to pick it up before it was stepped on. Scuffles broke out and Casey could see that tempers were frayed.

The Red Eyes looked on from behind their alien helmets, impassive. They kept their plasma rifles in their hands, though, just in case things got too lively.

"This isn't right!" Casey muttered, her body tensing with anger as she watched the chaotic scenes. "They're treating them like animals."

"Why ain't they fighting back?" Elite asked. "We need to do something…"

"We can't get involved," Cheeze warned. "Not here. Not right now. We don't have weapons or anything." He touched Casey's arm, warning her not to do anything rash.

"You're right." She swallowed back her fury. "We can't do anything until we know what's going on. Let's move on."

They headed back towards what was left of Big Ben, then onto Westminster Bridge towards the south side of the city. The River Thames, dirty and grey, flowed silently beneath them. There was no traffic on the bridge and some of the crowd from the food trucks had already begun to swarm in the same direction, overtaking Casey and her friends. A man on a bicycle whizzed past, ringing his bell to clear the way. His food package was securely tied into a basket on the handlebars, and he had a baseball bat resting on top of it in easy reach.

"Which way is your house?" Cheeze asked Casey, his hoverchair humming.

"A couple of miles south of the river. If we get there we can regroup and work out what to do for the best. Once we get across the bridge, it should be straightforward."

Fish pointed across the river. "Are you sure about that?"

Casey squinted up ahead, and her face fell. He was right. It didn't look like it was going to be straightforward at all.

2

PAPERS, PLEASE!

A huge metal wall divided Westminster Bridge in two. It was several metres high, made of solid black steel, and topped with coils of razor wire. CCTV cameras were fixed along its length, as well as two electronic display boards broadcasting a scrolling selection of propaganda slogans:

OBEY
PEACE & PROSPERITY
ARCTURIA ASCENDANT

A checkpoint gate was built into the middle of the wall manned by a squad of Red Eyes. Their reptilian faces were hidden behind their angular black helmets.

"Is this thing designed to keep people in or keep them out?" Cheeze asked, surveying the barrier.

"I reckon a bit of both," Casey replied, as a line of civilians, all clutching their food parcels, queued up at the checkpoint to get across to the south side of the city. Before they could pass through, they had to have their retinas checked and verified by a team of Red Cap soldiers armed with handheld scanners.

"If they scan us, they'll realize we're not on their system," Brain said.

"What do you think'll happen then, bruv?" Elite asked nervously.

"I'm guessing: *bang, bang, you're dead*," Cheeze replied drily, eyeing the aliens' plasma rifles.

Elite looked over the side of the bridge at the grey water churning below. "Could we swim for it?"

"The fall would probably kill us," Brain told him. "Then there's the currents, the cold."

"Plus, I can't swim," Fish confessed. "I'm scared of the water."

Elite sucked his teeth. "But your nickname's Fish…"

"Because my dad owns a chip shop, not because I'm part-salmon."

"It doesn't matter anyway," Casey interrupted. "Look!" She pointed down at the water where several black shapes floated.

Elite hung over the side of the bridge to get a better look. "What are they? Mines?"

"No idea, but I don't think any of us want to take a dip today."

As the team hesitated, an elderly woman approached. She was pushing a supermarket shopping trolley containing her food package. One of the wheels was slightly wonky and it kept veering sideways. As she neared them she clocked Cheeze's hoverchair and eyed it jealously.

"No wheels," she remarked. "Looks like magic." She stopped for a moment to catch her breath. "Where are you from?" she asked, looking them up and down.

"We're just visiting … from out of town," Fish said, letting his Glaswegian accent become even thicker than usual.

The woman fixed him with a beady stare through her heavily kohled lashes. "If you're not authorized, you'll never make it through the checkpoint," she warned. She looked over at Casey and her expression softened. "You remind me of my granddaughter. She was about your age when the Arcturians came."

"Is she…?" Casey began then stopped, uncertain how to ask the question that was forming on her lips.

"No, not dead. Sent to the work camps."

"Work camps?"

"Where have you been?" the woman asked with a frown. "On the moon?"

"Something like that," muttered Cheeze.

"The work camps are where they take people who resist. If you're really unlucky they send you to the digs." She paused, a thin smile pursing her lips. "I suppose you don't know what the digs are, either?"

"The Red Eyes are digging up pieces of the array," Brain said. "They must need manpower for it. Good way to keep people in their place, I guess."

"Ah, you're a smart one," the woman said, squinting at him. "Are you the leader of this little gang?"

Brain smiled, amused, and looked sideways at Casey.

"Oh, you are?" the old woman said, turning back to her. "What's your name, dear?"

"Casey."

"Pretty. Where are you trying to get to?"

"My mum's house. South of the river. Is there another bridge we can cross?"

The old woman shook her head. "It's the same on all the bridges. The whole city is divided up into sectors. You need permission to cross between them. Where exactly are you going?"

"Clapham Common."

"I live near there!" the woman replied. "Can I take a message to someone for you? What street is it?"

"Burton Str—" Casey started to say, then hesitated as Brain flashed her a look of warning.

"What number?" the woman asked, a little too insistent.

"You know what?" Brain said. "We'll take our chances. But thank you for the offer."

The woman looked ready to ask again but seemed to think better of it. "You're right to be careful," she said instead. "There are lots of spies around. They'll happily sell you out for a few extra ration points." She smiled thinly and, as she did, Casey noticed that her red lipstick had smeared onto her teeth. It looked like blood. "Good luck," she said and walked on, struggling to keep her shopping trolley in a straight line.

Casey looked around. The bridge was now packed with civilians, all impatient to get home with their food parcels.

"What should we do?" Elite asked, starting to panic.

Casey thought about the strange powers the Squids had unlocked for her. Could she use them here, on Earth? Bust open the checkpoint gate, maybe? Blast the Red Eyes across the bridge and escape? It seemed liked madness. Even if she dared, there was no way she could keep the boys safe while she did it. There were too many soldiers, too many guns. Someone would end up getting hurt.

She sighed, feeling the familiar weight of responsibility for her friends. The adventure on Hosin –

and the powers the Squids had given her – made her feel different from the boys. She couldn't help but notice the change in how they responded to her. Even Cheeze, who she was closer to than any of them, had started to look at her differently. She was no longer the shy girl they'd met in the shopping centre a few days ago.

She was awoken from her reverie by a sudden blast of music as the giant display boards above the barrier abruptly burst into life, the slogans wiped away as if someone had changed the channel. Two perky news presenters, a man and a woman, stared into the camera, their faces fixed with dazzling white smiles. They seemed to inhabit a totally different world to the haggard people queuing for food on the street.

"Good morning. This is your news update on the hour," the woman said. "Our Arcturian allies are celebrating the successful excavation of the latest piece of the psionic array."

The broadcast cut to footage of Red Eye troops in the Sahara Desert. They watched as human workers toiled in the heat. Casey recognized some of them as the *SkyWake* gamers she'd last seen on Hosin, the ones who'd been abducted and turned into unwilling soldiers by the Arcturians. They still wore the strange electronic devices on their heads that controlled their minds. Others seemed to be local people who'd been press-ganged into service. They used Arcturian equipment – futuristic-looking tools that resembled pneumatic drills and excavators – to dig a huge pit around an enormous triangular-shaped structure. Casey gasped as it came properly into view. It was the Great Pyramid in Egypt.

Beneath the pyramid, excavated from the sand, lay a strange, blue object. It looked like some kind of satellite antenna, although what its purpose was, deep below the ground, wasn't clear.

"This now marks the fifth discovery in our quest to uncover all the pieces of this ancient alien artefact," continued the newsreader. The screens filled with archive footage of the past digs – under ancient temples in the steamy jungles of Central America; beneath the giant stone heads on Easter Island in the Pacific; and around the Nazca Lines in the Peruvian Desert. It was as if every ancient wonder of the world hid a piece of this strange alien technology.

The footage cut again, this time to an ornate briefing room with wood-panelled walls. A lectern stood on a podium facing the camera. Two Union Jacks hung on poles on either side of it. As the Reapers watched, a young man stepped up to the lectern and faced the camera. Casey gasped. It was Xander, the YouTube streamer. He was four years older than when they'd last seen him. He'd let his hair grow long and he wore a small goatee beard. He was flanked by two Red Eyes in black power armour. Both carried plasma rifles, although quite what threat they were expecting to encounter in the TV studio wasn't clear.

"My fellow citizens," Xander said, spreading his arms wide. "Today our Arcturian allies completed a successful excavation of the new dig site and discovered the fifth part of the psionic array. Our chief technical officer is carrying out a full analysis of the latest artefact. He is confident that he will be able to pinpoint the sixth and final location in due course."

The camera panned slightly to reveal Pete standing in Xander's shadow. The boys all turned to look at Casey, but she just stared in horrified silence as her brother's face filled the screen. He was taller and more mature, no longer her baby brother. She struggled to get her head around the fact that he was now the same age as her, not to mention the realization that he was the "chief technical officer" to whom Xander was referring. He had clearly thrown in his lot with the Arcturians. A wave of fresh anger crashed over her. How could he have teamed up with Earth's enemies? She felt totally betrayed. This was unforgivable.

"With your help," Xander continued, "we will aid our allies in their quest. Their success is our success. For the glory of Arcturia!" He held his closed fist to his chest in imitation of the Arcturian salute and smiled that charming, yet totally insincere, smile that Casey had come to hate.

She turned to her teammates, hoping to let off a bit of steam. But they weren't watching. They were looking over their shoulders, back towards Big Ben. A squad of Red Eyes had just marched past the ruined clock tower and was now heading towards the bridge.

Cheeze gasped. "Get ready to rumble, guys. I think we're in trouble."

3
RESISTANCE ISN'T FUTILE

"We're trapped," Brain warned as the Red Eyes stepped onto Westminster Bridge. The team was sandwiched between the approaching aliens and the checkpoint gate. There was nowhere to run, no way to escape. The aliens spread out to form a line across the width of the bridge. They moved forward slowly, their black power armour glinting in the morning sunlight. As they advanced, they herded the remaining civilians towards the checkpoint.

"Do you reckon we could get through them?" Cheeze asked. "Head back to Big Ben and into the Tube tunnels?"

"They're pushing everyone this way," Casey said, her eyes never leaving them. "If we try to go back, it'll be like having a flashing neon sign above our heads saying: ARREST US."

"Then we jump and take our chances with the mines," Elite said. "Fish? Can you manage it? You can hold onto me." He turned to the Scottish boy, but his friend wasn't listening.

Fish was distracted by a girl ahead of them. She had frizzy red hair and wore combat trousers with black Doc Marten boots. The rest of the team followed his gaze and watched as the girl set a bulky rucksack down against the cast iron balustrades that lined the bridge's sides. She paused for a moment, looking out over the river as if taking in the view. Then she walked on to the checkpoint, keeping her eyes fixed straight ahead.

"She left her rucksack!" Fish exclaimed. He jogged towards it, keen to help. "Hey!" he shouted after the retreating girl. "You forgot your bag!"

"We don't have time for this," Brain frowned.

Casey checked over her shoulder. The approaching Red Eyes were getting closer. As she watched their progress, she noticed a Black teenager standing on the opposite side of the bridge. The boy was huge, the size of a mountain. He wore a green military surplus parka and carried a duffel bag over his shoulder. He unslung it and put it down under one of the ornate Victorian lampposts that lined the bridge. He then walked away nonchalantly without it, just like the girl had done.

"Something's happening…" Casey murmured.

By this time, Fish had reached the girl's rucksack. He picked it up, surprised by its weight. He needed both hands to haul it off the ground.

"Hey!" he called out after her, louder this time. "Miss!" The girl clocked him and cursed under her breath. She clearly didn't want the rucksack back. She pushed forward into the crowd of people waiting to enter the checkpoint gate, keen to get away.

"Hello!" Fish cried, oblivious. "I think this is yours!"

The commotion attracted attention. Two of the Red Eyes at the checkpoint broke ranks and headed over to see what was going on. They were joined by one of the human soldiers. The mysterious girl and boy vanished into the crowd separately, seemingly unnoticed by anyone apart from the Reapers.

"Drop the rucksack!" a Red Eye shouted at Fish in Arcturian, his jet-black helmet quickly translating the harsh, alien sounds in a mechanical voice.

The boy froze.

"Get down on the ground!" a Red Cap ordered, joining the stand-off.

"What do you want me to do first?" Fish asked sulkily, looking from the alien to the human. "Drop the rucksack or get on the ground?"

"Don't try to be funny," the Red Cap warned, pulling

a shock baton from his belt. The device crackled menacingly.

Fish swallowed hard, his defiant swagger evaporating. "OK, OK, keep your hair on," he muttered. "I'll just put this down—"

He didn't get to finish his sentence as the rucksack burst into life in his hands. The fabric ripped open and half a dozen Arcturian drones tore out of it and flew up into the sky. On the other side of the road, the same thing happened to the duffel bag. The twelve drones flew high above the bridge in looping circles, climbing and dipping like swifts in summer. Then, as the Red Eyes raised their rifles to open fire, the drones swooped down onto the bridge in an attack formation.

Panic erupted. The civilians stampeded in fright. The Red Eyes opened fire wildly, without any real hope of hitting anything. The drones weren't fitted with weapons, but their speed alone made them dangerous. One smashed into a Red Eye, decking him with the force of a heavyweight boxer delivering a knockout punch. The blow cracked the invader's helmet in two, revealing a scaly, reptilian face beneath it. The alien hissed in anger.

"Look out!" Casey shouted to her teammates as the drones swarmed over their heads. At the same moment, there was a roar of an engine. The military truck that had delivered the food parcels in Parliament Square was now gunning towards them, accelerating at top speed over the bridge towards the checkpoint. Everyone scattered to avoid it. As it thundered by, Casey glimpsed a boy – Asian, with a shock of dark hair and a stern face – behind the wheel. He didn't look like he was going to stop for anything.

"It's the Resistance!" a terrified man shouted as he dived out of the way. Casey caught sight of three more teens in the back of the truck as it passed, clinging on for dear life among the food ration packs.

The Red Eye who'd lost his helmet raised his plasma rifle. His forked tongue flickered between his lips as he lined up the truck in his sights. But before he could fire another drone swooped at him, knocking the gun out of his hands.

"Someone must have hacked them," Brain said, raising his eyebrows at Cheeze.

"Don't look at me," his friend cried, holding up his hands in innocence. "I didn't do it!"

There was an ear-splitting crunch of metal as the army truck smashed through the checkpoint gate, busting it wide open. The Red Eyes fired as it passed them, shooting indiscriminately. A man carrying a food package was hit in the back, his scream torn from his lips as a ball of plasma disintegrated him. Several bystanders dived off the bridge in panic. There were a series of explosions in the water as they triggered the floating mines.

Back on the bridge the red-haired girl reappeared from between the fleeing crowd. She dived across the tarmac and grabbed the downed Red Eye's plasma rifle. Firing steady blasts from the alien weapon she retreated through the checkpoint on foot, covering her friend who ran ahead of her. They hotfooted it to the waiting truck and jumped in the back. It pulled away in a cloud of diesel fumes.

Fish stared in open-mouthed wonder as it departed. "I think I'm in love," he whispered.

"Ghost Reapers, let's move!" Casey shouted, realizing that this was their best chance to escape. Until the Arcturians regained control of the bridge, no one needed to be scanned to cross to the south side of the city.

The team charged through the busted checkpoint alongside a crowd of fleeing civilians. Ahead of them the stolen truck disappeared around a corner, its tyres screeching on the tarmac. Casey didn't know who the Resistance were, but she was glad to see that at least someone was fighting back.

4

I HAVE A ROLLING PIN AND I'M NOT AFRAID TO USE IT

It was early evening by the time the Reapers finally made it to Casey's house. In the aftermath of the attack on the checkpoint, Red Cap foot patrols combed the rubble-strewn streets, stopping pedestrians to scan their faces and check their identities. It forced the Reapers to move slowly, keeping to the side streets and doubling back on themselves every now and then to avoid being stopped. Keen to blend in, they took out their phones so they could tap at the screens, like they'd seen other people doing as they played that game with the blocks.

"Do you think it's safe to message my fam?" Elite asked as he tapped at his phone. "Can I let them know we're back?"

"Better not," warned Brain. "Not until we know what's going on. The Red Eyes could be monitoring the phone system. You might give us all away."

"Seriously?" Fish interrupted. "Casey's getting to see her mum. Why can't we all call home?"

"We're only going to my house because it's the closest," Casey told him, feeling a little guilty. She couldn't imagine what she'd say if the situation was reversed. Suddenly she wanted more than anything to be home. To have a hug from her mum.

"C'mon, you guys," Fish said, looking around for support. "Surely you want to speak to your families too? We've been away for four years! Who knows what's happened to them while we were gone?"

Casey didn't feel she should voice an opinion on what they should do, although her gut told her that Brain was right to be cautious. Who knew if the Red Eyes would be tracking people's phone calls or not? They definitely ruled everything with an iron grip. Yet it was only natural her friends would want to speak to their families.

She thought back to what she knew of the boys' home lives from when they used to play *SkyWake* online together. Brain lived in Leeds with his parents, who were consultants at the local hospital. Fish's dad and brothers were in Glasgow. Cheeze was from the Midlands but never really said much about his family. Elite, she knew, was from South London, like her, though a bit further out.

"We don't have to go to my house," she told them as they crossed the street. "Elite lives in London too, right? We could go to his place."

The team sniper nodded. "Yeah," he said, then frowned. "But I live in a two-bed near the top of a tower block. Not sure we're all gonna fit in there, and we'd be spotted heading up the staircase together." He paused a moment. "Plus, I've got a little sister. She'll be, like, seven now. If we're getting chased by Red Eyes, I don't want to mess things up for her. Put her in danger, like? You feel me?"

Casey nodded. "It's probably just my mum at our house. Maybe Pete too." She saw how the boys shifted uncomfortably at the mention of her brother's name. He'd betrayed them just as much as her.

Half an hour later, they arrived on Casey's street. It looked nothing like she remembered. A good third of the houses had been flattened, demolished in the invasion. Parked cars sat here and there, covered in grime and fallen leaves, as if they hadn't been used for years. The tall conker trees that once lined the pavements had been roughly chopped down. Stacks of logs lay in the front gardens, waiting to be taken inside. Several chimneys belched out smoke and the air was thick with the smell of burning wood.

Casey stopped outside her front gate, glad to see her

house had survived the destruction. It seemed different. Maybe it had got smaller. Or she had got bigger. She knew that her adventure, from Earth to Hosin and back again, had changed her. She was no longer the same girl she'd been when she'd stepped out of the door to go to the eSports tournament.

She paused. Was she even the same age any more? The thought jolted her. They'd lost four years on their return to Earth, spinning through hyperspace as the navigation computer on the shuttle malfunctioned. It felt like she'd left to go to the eSports tournament just days ago, but as far as Earth was concerned it had been four years. Her head spun.

"We should get inside," Brain said, interrupting her thoughts. He scanned the street nervously.

The key for the front door was still in its usual hiding place, inside a fake plastic rock in the front garden. Casey paused as she slotted it into the front door. She'd wanted to be back here so badly ever since they'd left the shopping centre. But now that she was, everything felt messed up.

She forced herself to turn the key and crept inside, keeping the lights off for fear of attracting attention. Cheeze's hoverchair scratched the skirting boards in the dim hallway as he manoeuvred along it into the open plan kitchen. No one was home.

"Right," Brain said, taking a seat on the bar stools around the island in the middle of the kitchen. "We need to work out what we're doing."

"I just want to speak to my dad," Fish said. He pulled his dead phone from his pocket and plugged it into the socket by the kettle to charge. "I need to check my brothers are all right."

"Maybe messaging's safer?" Elite suggested.

"We don't know what's safe and what isn't," Cheeze mused, rubbing his forehead. "Maybe we should wait until Casey's mum gets home. Where is she, anyway?"

"She's doing a late shift at the hospital," Casey said, flicking through the papers stuck on the noticeboard. "Her rota's here. She should be back soon."

"Your mum got any scran?" Fish asked, looking around the kitchen. The remains of an empty food ration pack, like the ones the Red Caps had given out to the civilians, sat on the counter. Casey opened a few cupboards. They were unusually bare. The only thing in the fridge was an out-of-date jar of mustard. Even the fruit bowl, which her mum always liked to keep stocked in an attempt to entice her children to eat healthily, was empty. That never happened.

Closing the fridge, Casey noticed a family photo stuck on the door. Her and Pete standing side by side on a beach in Wales in summer sunshine. It was the year she'd taught her brother how to bodyboard, just after their dad had died. She remembered how he struggled into his wetsuit and the yelp of joy he gave the first time he properly caught a wave. The photo was like a snapshot from another life. She stared into Pete's face a moment. He looked so young, so innocent. It was hard to believe he was working with the Arcturian invaders. She felt a sudden urge to rip the picture in half and separate herself from him for ever.

A noise outside interrupted her. Headlights shone in the darkness of the street. A car door slammed.

"Wait here," she told the boys and crept into the shadowy living room. Through the window she could see two black SUVs pull up on the street outside. Four Red Caps stepped out, plasma rifles strapped across their chests. They checked the street with the watchful eyes of professional soldiers, scanning for danger. When they seemed satisfied it was all clear, a Red Cap opened the rear door of the second SUV.

Casey gasped at the sight of her mum climbing out of the backseat. She was wearing her nursing scrubs and had her hair tied in a bun like she always did when she was on shift. She looked tired. A man followed her out. He was dressed in black combat gear like the Red Caps, although he didn't look like any kind of soldier. He was short and bald with a beer belly that fought against the constraints of his uniform. He breezed past the Red Caps and opened the front gate for Casey's mum with a chivalrous flourish. Casey shrank back, watching their conversation through a chink in the curtain.

"Thank you for the lift home, Commander Deacon." Mum was much taller than the commander and towered over him.

"Always a pleasure to assist our brave NHS workers," the commander said. "Especially with so many reports of Resistance activity on the streets. But, please, call me Herbert."

Casey's mum paused on the front step as she fished for her house keys in her bag. "I do hope you manage to find the people who are causing all the problems."

"We will, we will, we always do," Commander Deacon assured her with a thin smile. He paused expectantly then, when he saw she wasn't going to say anything else, he added: "Would it be an imposition to invite myself in? For a cup of tea, perhaps?"

Casey froze. If he came inside, they'd be discovered for sure.

"I'm afraid I'm all out of tea," she heard her mum say. "And milk, too. Pretty much everything, in fact. I haven't had a chance to get my food rations today. I've been working triple shifts at the hospital."

There was a pause. "Oh, no," said Commander

Deacon. "That's no good. That's no good at all. Let me arrange a special delivery for you. As you know, I'm in charge of logistics for the district. All supplies come through me."

"Really?" Mum said. "I had no idea."

Casey knew her mum well enough to know she was lying.

"You'll have a delivery tomorrow," the commander continued firmly. "And then perhaps we can have that cup of tea? I might even be able to rustle up a packet of biscuits."

"I do love chocolate bourbons," Casey's mum said, her voice bubbly with an excitement that Casey could tell was fake. "While you're at it, could you also arrange a restock for the pharmacy at the hospital? Our last two deliveries didn't arrive and we're running short on antibiotics. Or maybe your power doesn't stretch that far?"

If her intention was to make the commander rise to the challenge, it worked. "My dear Rebecca," he blustered, "I handle *everything* in the district. Food, medicines, even weapons. Let me stop by the hospital tomorrow and you can tell me exactly what you need. Perhaps in return you'll do me the honour of joining me this Saturday?"

"Join you? What for?"

"At a very special gathering. I can't say too much about it, but it's an *exclusive* event. Black tie, champagne, the full monty. I'd be delighted to have you as my plus one." He chuckled to himself, although it wasn't clear what the joke was.

"I'll have to check I'm not on shift," Mum told him.

"Of course," the commander replied shortly. "It would be lovely if you could attend, though. We could discuss how to ensure that the hospital receives a regular supply of everything it needs." He paused a moment to let that sink in. "Goodnight, Rebecca."

He clicked his heels together, bowed, and kissed the back of her hand like a Prussian count. Then, without another word, he turned to his men and twirled his finger in the air in a helicopter motion. The Red Caps escorted him to his SUV. There wasn't any helicopter as far as Casey could see.

While her mum fumbled with her house keys, Casey tiptoed back to the kitchen. She wasn't sure what she'd just witnessed. Was her mum working with the invaders too, like Pete? Or was she somehow trying to trick the commander into giving her what she wanted?

The boys waited in the dark in anxious silence. They'd heard every word.

"She got rid of him," Casey told them. "But we'd better hide. If she comes in and sees all of us, she's likely to scream the place down. We don't want that creep charging in here with a squad of Red Caps trying to be her hero."

The boys nodded and grabbed hiding places. Brain and Elite shut themselves in the utility room. Cheeze moved his hoverchair into the cupboard under the stairs. Fish, unable to decide, found himself trapped in the middle of the kitchen as the key sounded in the front door. He dived behind the island. Even he knew it was a rubbish hiding place.

Casey's mum stepped into the hallway and turned on the lights. She kicked off her Crocs and let out a heavy sigh. Hidden behind the kitchen door, Casey watched as she dropped her keys in the bowl on the island. She looked worn out, her shoulders were stooped and her skin pale. The last time Casey had seen her like this was after her dad had died. She couldn't imagine what her mum had been through over the last four years. Losing both her children via alien abduction; watching the Earth being invaded; and then seeing her youngest child help the aliens while her eldest was missing, presumed dead, in deep space... It would be enough to finish anyone off.

The tap turned on and Mum poured herself a glass of water. She stood at the sink to drink it, her back to the room. Casey wondered how she could announce her presence without giving her a heart attack. She wanted to be absolutely sure the Red Caps had gone before she revealed herself.

Hello, Mum, it's me!
Scream! Crash!
Red Caps running in to see what was happening.
Guns. Shooting.
Game Over.

She decided to wait until her mum had put down the glass. As she hesitated, she saw Fish peering over the kitchen island. He mouthed silently at her, wanting to find a better hiding place. Casey shook her head impatiently, waving at him to stay low.

Mum placed the glass in the sink and turned around just as Fish ducked back into cover. She walked to the far side of the kitchen and rummaged inside a drawer before pulling out a wooden rolling pin. She hefted it in her hand.

She's baking? Casey thought to herself. *At this time of night? She doesn't even have any ingredients.*

"Whoever's in here better show themselves RIGHT NOW!" Mum said sternly, gripping the rolling pin and glaring around the kitchen. "I don't have any money and I don't have any food. But I do have a rolling pin and I'm not afraid to use it."

Fish popped his head up over the counter.

"Er, hello..." he said.

Mum eyeballed him, giving him what Casey used to call Stern Expression #2. It was enough to make Fish tremble. He backed away with his hands up. Casey realized it was time to reveal herself. She just hoped her mum didn't scream. But as she tried to emerge from her hiding place, she realized she was stuck. Her mum had slipped the rubber stopper under the door, inadvertently trapping Casey behind it.

Across the kitchen, Brain and Elite stuck their heads out of the utility room. Mum fixed them with a basilisk stare too.

"You two stay right there," she ordered, pointing her rolling pin at them like it was a loaded weapon. There was a rumble from the hallway and Cheeze came into the kitchen in his hoverchair.

"Hi, Mrs Henderson," he said chirpily, before realizing he'd timed his entrance badly. "Oh!"

"Who *are* you?" Mum demanded. "And what are you all doing in my house?'

"They're with me," Casey said, barging the stuck kitchen door open and almost falling flat on her face in the process.

Mum spun around at the sound of her daughter's voice. The rolling pin fell from her hand and clattered across the kitchen floor. She rushed over to Casey, wrapped her arms around her, and swept her into the biggest hug. Her body shook with silent sobs as she clutched her long-lost daughter tight.

"Casey!"

5

DON'T CALL US, WE'LL CALL YOU

It took over an hour for Casey to tell her mum everything that had happened, especially since the rest of the Ghost Reapers kept chipping in with details she'd forgotten. Mum listened in horror as Casey described the abductions in the shopping centre; she cheered as she heard how Casey blew up Scratch with her own plasma rifle; gasped as she learned about her children's arrival on Hosin; and burst into tears when Casey explained how Pete had decided to work with the aliens. By the time Casey told her about saving the Squids and the strange telepathic powers the aliens had helped her unlock, Mum was a wreck.

"Incredible, just incredible," she muttered as she hugged her daughter again, struggling to take it all in. Then she hugged the rest of the Reapers, too, ignoring Fish's half-hearted complaints.

Afterwards it was Mum's turn to tell the gamers her story. She explained how the first Red Eye dropships had arrived over the city four years earlier, while the world was still in shock over the abduction of the gamers from the *SkyWake* tournaments. The aliens' orbital command station had appeared in the sky above the Earth, watching over everything like an all-seeing eye.

The Reapers were amazed to hear how quickly the Earth had fallen. The aliens had launched a wave of attacks across the globe using the mind-controlled *SkyWake*rs from Hosin as their shock troops. Faced with children armed with plasma rifles and energy shields, the authorities were paralysed. They didn't know what to do.

"It's such a smart strategy," Brain said, nodding. "No one would want to fight against kids."

"But why didn't anyone attack the dropships or the space station?" Casey asked, unable to disguise her irritation at the failure of the planet to defend itself.

"The Red Eyes were too powerful," Mum explained, shivering at the memory. "You've seen what they did to London. They destroyed cities all over the globe. 'Shock and awe', the newspapers called it. After a couple of weeks, the world's richest men gathered and essentially agreed to work with the invaders. The tech billionaires cared more about protecting their fortunes than they did about protecting their planet. They put pressure on the United Nations to agree a ceasefire. Before we knew what was happening, Earth had officially surrendered. No vote, no referendum, no debate. Just a deal between the billionaires and the invaders. When it was done, the aliens sent the *SkyWaker*s to work at the first dig site. They didn't need them as soldiers any more."

"We sold out?" Casey asked, shaken. She couldn't believe what she was hearing.

"People decided that it was better to work with the Arcturians than fight them," Mum replied.

"That's grown-up speak for sold out," Casey fumed, her voice tight. "Why didn't anyone resist?"

"Some of us did," Mum protested. "In the first weeks after the ceasefire there was lots of pushback against the plans. We demonstrated and marched and occupied the streets. Soldiers and police officers and MPs joined us too. It didn't do any good, though. Most people just wanted things to go back to normal. They thought that working with the Arcturians would do that. There was so much propaganda on social media and in the newspapers. Plus, that boy Xander was on TV every night promising that if we helped the aliens find what they were looking for, they'd look after us. Lots of people believed him. Some still do…"

Mum paused, fighting back tears.

"What is it?" Casey asked, taking her hand.

"What happened to your brother while you were away?" Mum asked, her voice trembling. "When he came home he was totally different. Sullen and secretive, and constantly conspiring with Xander. Red Caps used to come to the house and whisk Pete off to meetings who-knows-where. I begged him not to go, but he told me not to worry. He said he knew what he was doing. Then, one day, he left, and he didn't come home again. I was frantic with worry. I spoke to the Red Caps, and they said he was staying with Xander in a luxury residence across the city. He's never even called me. I see him on television at night and I think to myself, *Is it him? Is that really my son?*"

Casey swallowed hard. "Pete made his own choices. I almost died trying to keep him safe from the Red Eyes, but he didn't want to listen to me."

"Casey did everything she could, Mrs Henderson," Cheeze told her, defending his friend. "She was a hero, just like your husband. She saved all of us."

"True dat," Elite agreed.

"It just doesn't make any sense," Mum whispered. "Why would Pete choose to help the aliens? Why wouldn't he come home to me?"

"Because he's changed," Casey snapped. "He's been seduced by Xander and all his 'for the win' nonsense.

Maybe if you weren't so busy getting romanced by turncoat soldiers, you could have stopped him."

"You mean Commander Deacon?" Mum scoffed. "I can assure you, young lady, I am not about to be romanced by the likes of *him*."

"He invited you to a fancy party!"

"Casey, look at me. I haven't worn a cocktail dress since 1997! Can you really see me hobnobbing over champagne and caviar?"

Casey couldn't help but smile at this.

"He's in charge of the biggest supply warehouse in the city," Mum continued. "The hospital is on its knees. There's not enough food, not enough medicine, not enough staff. We're close to collapse. I'm just trying to get the things we need to survive. That's all any of us are doing … *surviving*."

"But why isn't anyone fighting?" Casey demanded. "Why isn't anyone leading a counterattack or something?"

"There's no one left to lead. The Arcturians control everything. It's a constant battle just to get enough to eat and, even if you do, it's just nutritional paste and a few basics like bread and milk. Petrol is rationed, gas and electricity, too. The rich get all the luxuries. Meanwhile, the aliens stay up on their space station where we can't even attack them."

"There must be someone?"

Mum shook her head. "People are scared. If you put a foot out of line, the Red Caps come after you. They're like the Arcturians' secret police. They keep everyone in order … and get well paid for it too. They're heartless."

"That's rough," Elite said and blew out his cheeks. "I'm thinking I'd better check in on my fam. See if they're OK."

"You should all go home," Mum agreed. "All of you. Your parents must be so worried about you."

The team looked at one another uncertainly.

"Wait, we can't just give up," Cheeze said, spinning his hoverchair away from the counter. "The Squids told us we had to stop the Red Eyes from activating the array and taking over the galaxy. If we don't, who else will?"

Casey ran her hand through her hair. She could see how tired and overwhelmed the boys were. She sensed Fish and Elite in particular weren't sure about any of it. None of them had expected their return to Earth to be like this. What could the five of them do against a whole planet? It seemed like a suicide mission.

"Mum's right," Casey whispered. "This isn't a team mission any more. It's something I have to do on my own. I mean, I'm the one the Squids gave the powers to. If I can find the array and work out what to do…" Her voice trailed off.

"No way you can do this without us!" Cheeze cried, his nostrils flaring in indignation. "Brain, tell her!"

Brain cleared his throat and pushed his glasses up his nose. "I think we need to reach out to the Resistance," he said. "Maybe they can help us."

"Don't get mixed up with the Resistance," Mum warned, her face clouding.

"We met some of them on the way here," Casey told her. "They stole a truck full of food."

"Typical!" Mum said, shaking her head. "All they do is wind up the invaders. They're just troublemakers, always stealing food and supplies. Do you know what happens to troublemakers? They get sent to work camps, or forced to dig up pieces of the array at the excavation sites like slaves. It's hard work. The Red Eyes are merciless and not everyone survives. You don't want that to happen to you or your families, do you?"

The boys shifted uncomfortably.

"You should go home," Casey told her friends. She was terrified of being left to do this on her own, but she didn't want them to have to make sacrifices for her. "Go and find your dad and brothers, Fish. Find your little sister, Elite. Look out for them."

"What about you, though?" Cheeze asked.

"I'll be fine," Casey lied. "I'll find the Resistance and maybe I can work something out with them."

Feeling tears welling up, she turned on her heel and headed out of the room. In the hallway she opened the door that led into the garage and stepped into the darkness. Safe in the gloom she choked out a silent sob. It was all too much, she decided. She felt overwhelmed. She stood there for a minute or two, letting her grief empty out of her. Then, as her wet eyes adjusted to the shadows, she saw it.

The *Space Invaders* cabinet.

It sat against the far wall, wrapped in an old tarpaulin. She pulled the cover off, disturbing a thick layer of dust that made her cough. The machine's colourful artwork was exactly as she remembered it. The huge furry alien monsters on the side panelling and the bright yellow font that spelled out the game's title were strangely comforting. She ran her fingers over the buttons on the front, remembering what it was like to play it.

Space Invaders was the game that had brought her to this point, she realized, not *SkyWake*. This retro arcade game about fighting an endless onslaught of aliens had been her inspiration and, in a way, her guide. She let her hands rest on the controls a moment, thinking about her dad. She felt a shiver of connection as if some invisible thread linking them was being pulled taut as the past reached out to the present. She missed him so much.

"Dad?" a voice whispered, making her jump.

She turned to see Fish entering the garage. He'd snuck in from the hallway without realizing she was here. He had his mobile phone against his ear. "It's me," he continued, his voice breaking slightly. He snivelled. "I'm OK, yeah. Are you? What about James and Malcolm?" There was a pause. "I'm so glad you're all OK."

Fish saw Casey standing in the corner. He gasped and dropped the phone. It crunched as it landed on the concrete. "Dad? Are you still there?" he said, grabbing it and putting it back to his ear.

"I didn't mean to scare you," Casey said, apologetic. "Is it broken?"

"It's dead," Fish said, tapping at the cracked screen. "I had to call them," he explained defensively. "I couldn't wait any longer. I just needed to know they were still alive. Ow!" He yelped as a sliver of glass from the cracked phone screen jabbed into his fingertip.

"Here," Casey said, taking his hand. "Let me see." She carefully pulled out the glass with the tips of her nails. Her teammate sucked at the bloody pinprick it left behind.

"What are you doing out here, anyway?" Fish asked.

"I was just thinking things over."

The boy gasped as he noticed the *Space Invaders*

machine behind her. "Wow! Is that an original?" He walked over and rested his hands on the buttons on the front panel. "Where's the joystick?"

"No joystick. Just buttons. Left, right, fire. That's all you need. I guess it's pretty basic."

"No, it's not! This is like gaming history right here. Can we play it? Does it work?" He looked around the back and found the power cable. It was still plugged into the wall. "Can I turn it on?"

Casey hesitated, uncertain about revisiting this game. It meant so much to her. She wasn't sure she was ready for the emotions it would stir up. Fish was eager and, oblivious to her pause, he flicked the switch. The cabinet hummed as the game powered up.

At the same moment, everything erupted. Car tyres screeched to a stop on the street outside. Boots hit tarmac, voices shouted, and there was a rattle of guns.

"What did I do?" Fish cried in fright, staring at the power socket as if flicking the switch had triggered all the commotion.

"They're here!" Casey shouted and dragged him back into the house.

6

"COME OUT WITH YOUR HANDS UP!"

"We're surrounded!" Brain warned Casey and Fish as they came back into the living room. He was peering through the front window, trying to stay hidden. A dozen unmarked cars had pulled up outside the house, flashing lights illuminating the street. A squad of soldiers jumped out of the vehicles. They wore black combat outfits and the distinctive berets that gave them their name.

"Red Caps!" Mum cried.

"More out back," Elite hissed from the kitchen, as he watched another squad of troops scale the wall at the bottom of the garden. "How did they find out we were here?"

Casey paused, unwilling to get Fish into trouble.

"It's my fault," he sighed, keen to confess. "I—"

He didn't get to finish the sentence.

"Look!" Brain cried, pointing out of the front

window where an old lady with a shopping trolley was animatedly talking to the Red Caps, her phone in her hand. It was the woman from the checkpoint. One of the soldiers tapped his phone and the woman's handset lit up. She checked the screen and smiled, satisfied.

Elite ran his hand through his hair. "That grandma ratted us out!"

"People are so desperate for food they'll sell out their own neighbours for a few extra ration points," Casey's mum explained bitterly.

"Is that why everyone's playing that weird game on their phones?"

Mum nodded. "If you don't play it, you don't get rations. No one knows why it's such a big deal, but the Arcturians are making everyone play it every day. It's really hard on older people like her. They're struggling to score enough points, because they're not used to games or even smartphones and their reaction times aren't that fast any more. It's cruel."

Casey watched as the Red Caps closed in. Several took up position on the street, guns pointing towards the front door over the bonnets of their vehicles. Two imposing Arcturian soldiers hung back, watching the raid unfold, happy to let the humans do the hard work. Their black polished power armour reflected the flashing blue lights.

"This is the police," a voice shouted. "We have the building surrounded. Surrender your weapons!"

"What weapons, bruv?" Elite muttered. "We don't have nothing."

Brain looked around the room, panic in his eyes. "Is there another way out of here?"

"They're already covering the back," Cheeze told him. "It won't be long before they storm the place."

"The roof!" Casey exclaimed suddenly. "There's a skylight on the roof."

Mum grabbed her arm. "Casey, you can't keep fighting. You have to give yourselves up before someone gets seriously hurt. This isn't a game. Let me speak to them. I'll tell them you're unarmed and that you'll come out one by one. Please, I don't want to lose you again."

Casey paused, then nodded.

"Just make sure they don't hurt my friends."

"Good girl," Mum said, patting her arm. "We'll sort this out somehow, I promise." She headed towards the front door.

The boys looked at one another in confusion.

"You're surrendering?" Cheeze whispered, incredulous. "After all we've been through?"

"Listen to me," Casey said quietly, looking each boy in the eye. "I don't want anything to happen to you guys. You're going to give yourselves up to the Red

Caps. I'm going to make a run for it. I know this isn't how you want things to end, but it's for the best. I have to do this on my own."

"You mean you're ditching us?" Elite demanded, sounding small and hurt. "I thought we were a team!"

"Yeah," Fish complained. "Don't we even get a say? You're being really…" He paused. "Look, I know it's rude to say this to a girl and everything." He looked sideways at Cheeze for support, but his friend just grimaced in warning. "But you're being really *bossy*…"

The others took a deep inward breath.

"You can't call her that, bruv," Elite hissed. "It's, like, a stereotype."

"No one ever calls boys bossy," Cheeze agreed.

Casey reddened. "I'm trying to get you home safely," she snapped, unable to hide her frustration. "You have to get back to your families. They need you. If that makes me bossy, then…" She waved her hand in frustration. "Fine!"

While they argued, Mum headed down the hallway and started to open the front door. Realizing they were out of time, Casey raced past her and ran up the stairs, two at a time.

"Casey, wait! Stay here!" Mum cried.

At the same moment there was a commotion as two Red Caps tried to barge their way through the door.

Mum put her weight behind it, and the security chain clattered as it was pulled taut.

Upstairs, Casey ran past her bedroom, barely even registering the WARNING: NO STUPID PEOPLE BEYOND THIS POINT sign that hung on her door, and then flew up the twisty staircase into the loft extension. She could hear her mum arguing with the Red Caps through the gap in the front door, begging for leniency for her daughter and her friends.

At the top of the house, Casey jumped onto her parents' bed and reached for the skylight. As she began to pull it open, she heard footsteps behind her and turned, expecting to be met with plasma rifles. How had the soldiers got in already? But it was the Reapers.

"We're coming with you," Brain told her, panting for breath. Fish and Elite were close on his heels. "No arguments. We're not going home until this is over."

Downstairs, Casey's mum screamed as the front door was kicked open and the security chain broke. Several Red Caps thundered up the stairs in pursuit of the Reapers. Brain pulled the wardrobe over the bedroom door as a makeshift barricade. As he did, an old golf bag fell out and hit the floor. Casey recognized it as her dad's.

"This won't hold them long," Brain warned, looking at the flimsy wardrobe. "Grab a weapon." He picked up a golf club and tossed it to Elite, then found another for Fish.

"Hey, this is a putter!" the sandy-haired boy complained, looking at the paltry club he'd been thrown. "What am I supposed to do with this? Play crazy golf?"

Ignoring them, Casey pulled herself up through the skylight and climbed out onto the sloping tiles of the roof. She felt her stomach flip as she balanced herself, trying not to look at the street far below her. One misstep and she'd fall to certain injury, maybe death. She cast her eyes towards the night sky to fight off her vertigo. As she did, she saw the outline of the orbital command platform high above the Earth. The Red Eyes really were everywhere.

One by one, the boys pulled themselves through the skylight and balanced beside her on the tiles.

"Now what?" Fish asked, looking around in fear.

"We're going to have to make a jump for the next roof," Casey said, assessing the gap between her house and the neighbour's. "Where's Cheeze?" she asked, suddenly realizing they were one Reaper short.

"He said he was going to create a distrac—"

There was a crash down below as their friend's hoverchair burst out of the garage, ripping the metal door off its brackets. Cheeze had raised the chair's shield and its inbuilt plasma rifle was blasting left and right, sending aliens and humans alike ducking for cover. He spun his chair around and barrelled down the street, drawing their fire.

Casey saw one of the Red Eyes speak into the communicator on his power suit. She guessed he was calling for reinforcements.

"Let's go!" she shouted to her friends. It was only a metre or so from their roof to the next one, a jump that was more daunting than impossible. Before she could attempt it, though, an Arcturian drone appeared in the gap between the two houses and hung in the air blocking her way. Casey pulled up short.

"Watch out!" Elite yelled as he crashed into her back. The two friends struggled to keep their balance on the sloped roof. The drone bobbed in front of them and extended a menacing prong that crackled with electrical energy.

"I've got this!" Fish yelled somewhere behind them. "*Fore!*"

There was a crack as Fish rushed forward and hit the drone head-on with his golf putter, smashing its fisheye camera lens. The force of the blow knocked the machine into a tailspin. It dropped out of the sky like a stone and plummeted into a greenhouse in next door's garden.

"Hole in one!" Fish cheered, throwing the now-broken putter aside.

Before anyone could congratulate him, there was a heavy thud and the whole street shook. The four Ghost Reapers looked across the rooftops. Moving across the open green space of Clapham Common strode an enormous futuristic machine. It had three long, thin legs and a curved metal body that was as smooth and polished as a beetle's carapace. It stepped towards them jerkily, its hydraulics emitting a screeching howl that made their blood run cold.

7

HOW MANY LEGS DOES A TRIPOD HAVE?

"What the hell *is* that thing?" Elite cried as the giant alien walking machine approached. It stepped over the rooftops around the edge of the common as if they were dollhouses. Casey guessed from the presence of a cockpit slung underneath it that there was a pilot somewhere inside, directing it towards them.

"It must be something they've designed while we were away," Brain said, cocking his head on one side and appraising it like it was a science exhibit rather than a machine that might obliterate them at any moment. "Impressive."

"Shock and awe," Casey murmured, remembering what her mum had called the Arcturian tactic of scaring the Earth into submission with superior firepower. How could anyone hope to fight back against something this big?

A searchlight on the machine's undercarriage flicked on, illuminating the Reapers as they balanced on the roof. Casey shielded her eyes from the searing beam and, as she did, she heard the machine's plasma cannons swivel towards them.

"It might be impressive, but it's not taking prisoners!" she warned. "Move!" She grabbed Elite, who was standing nearest, and pulled him down onto the tiles beside her. The pair of them slid down the sloping roof on their backsides, picking up speed at a frightening pace before flying over the guttering into the air. The flat roof of a single storey extension below them broke their fall, although the impact hurt far more than Casey had expected. Another set of bruises to add to her growing collection.

Fish and Brain landed beside them a moment later, in a jumble of limbs. There was no time to complain because the walking machine was now blasting the roof they'd just been standing on. The tiles disintegrated and the wooden rafters quickly caught fire, the flames tinged green with Arcturian plasma.

Casey and the boys jumped off the extension into the garden below and crouched among the patio furniture.

"Where to?" Brain asked. There was a shed at the far end of the garden and an ornamental pond in the middle of the lawn, but not a lot else. Somewhere nearby a dog barked angrily, annoyed by the commotion.

"Can we grab weapons from the shed?" Fish suggested.

Elite shook his head. "Gonna take more than a Flymo to bring that thing down."

The patio shook as the machine appeared above the burning roof of the house, its searchlight shining into the garden. The light illuminated the ornamental pond, prompting a few koi carp to smack their lips at the surface of the water as they tried to work out if dawn had come early.

"We've got to make a run for it," Casey hissed, pointing towards the fence at the bottom of the garden.

"That thing'll blast us if we move," Fish fretted.

"It'll blast us if we stay, bruv," countered Elite.

"On the count of three," Casey said. They were out of the machine's sights at the moment, but it would only be a matter of time before it found them.

"Wait!" Fish hissed. "Do we go on three, or after three?"

"What?" Casey asked.

"One, two, THREE! Or one, two, three, GO!"

Brain glared at him. "Does it matter?"

"Every second counts."

"Then why are we wasting time discussing this?!"

The machine moved forward, its legs smashing through the burning house as if it was nothing more than cardboard. It twisted its body left and right looking for them.

"*Onetwothreego!*" Casey shouted and darted forward. The boys followed. The pilot opened fire as the teammates sprinted across the lawn. Plasma ripped through the garden, setting the grass and shrubs on fire and broiling the unfortunate fish in the pond.

Casey and the boys jumped over the fence at the bottom of the garden and found themselves on another suburban street. Cheeze appeared beside them, his hoverchair's shields up to give them some protection.

It was pretty obvious that they didn't have a hope of escaping. The giant machine was already chasing after them, shaking the ground as it ran. Its weapons jerked, preparing for another shot.

"Keep running!" Casey shouted. As the boys sped away she spun around and turned to face their pursuer. She stood on the dotted white line in the middle of the street and pulled herself up to her full height, staring the machine down as it pounded towards her. She felt like an ant trying to stop an elephant. Something about the unfairness of it incensed her. How dare the Red Eyes chase her friends like this, after all they'd been through to get back home?

She thought of Dreyfus, Private Ross and Eldreth the Squid. They'd all given their lives trying to help her. She thought of the Arcturians' endless attempts to destroy Hosin and then of her brother's betrayal.

A wave of fury washed over her, hot fire pumping through her veins.

The machine paused and looked down at her, its targeting systems locking on. The cockpit had black-tinted windows, making it impossible to see who was inside. She guessed that whoever it was couldn't believe that this tiny human was standing in their way. She was grateful for the extra second or two their hesitation gave her. She could already feel that strange power – flow, or whatever it was – rising within her. She remembered the Squid ability that *SkyWake* players called Telekinesis. She just hoped she could do something useful with it.

She looked at the two rows of parked cars that ran along the street. As she lifted her hands into the air, a car on either side of her levitated above the tarmac. One of them, a jet-black Audi, started to screech as its alarm system mistook the vehicle's sudden departure from the ground as a sign that it was being stolen. The horn blared and the hazard warning lights flashed on and off as the vehicle hovered unsteadily in mid-air.

With a frown of concentration and a swift upward motion of her hands, Casey sent the Audi hurtling towards the Red Eye machine, then threw the second car after it for good measure. The two vehicles crashed into the machine's smooth body, knocking it sideways just as it opened fire. The leg hydraulics compensated for the impact with a jerk and a shriek, but the cannon fire went perilously wide. Before the machine could right itself, Casey screamed in anger and raised two more cars off the ground. She hurled them, too, amazed by her power. But she knew, deep down, that this wasn't nearly enough to defeat this enormous enemy.

The alien machine was ready for her this time. It locked onto the two cars as they flew through the air and blasted them with its plasma cannons. They exploded with a percussive *whompf* that seemed to suck all the air out of the street.

The blast knocked Casey onto the tarmac. She lay there for a moment, surrounded by the burning debris from the vehicles, stunned. The heat was intense. She felt the strange power fading away. Not for the first time, she wished that she'd stayed with the Squids and learned how to use this mysterious ability properly.

Satisfied that this girl was no longer a threat, the machine turned its attention back to her friends. Two metal cables flew from its undercarriage and whipped down the street after the escaping boys. The first knocked Cheeze's hoverchair, sending it spinning off course. The second wrapped itself around Brain's waist and hoisted him into the air, shaking him left and right before releasing him. The boy flew through the air and crashed into a bush in a front garden, his already battered spectacles spinning off his face. Fish and Elite ran to help him. Casey, still lying in the road, looked on helplessly. They had no hope against something this big.

There was a sudden screech of tyres, as a grubby Luton van – once white, but now covered in a patina of city grime – zoomed out of a side street. The words CLEAN ME! had been scrawled in the dirt along its side by a cheeky finger. The van did a tight doughnut in front of the walking machine, spinning around so its rear cargo door was facing the giant enemy. There was a clatter as the roller shutter flew up and a petite teenage girl jumped out. She wore a baseball cap and carried a long metal tube that was taller than her.

"Get down!" she yelled. In a swift motion, she dropped to one knee and lifted the tube onto her shoulder. Casey recognized it from *SkyWake*. It was a Jackhammer, the Arcturian answer to a rocket-propelled grenade launcher.

THWUMP! A projectile flew out of the tube, almost knocking the petite girl over with its force. The rocket flew through the night air, spinning in a circle as it raced towards the giant Red Eye walking machine. The pilot opened fire in response – but too late. The giant contraption let out a shrill shriek as the rocket exploded against its side. It sounded like a cry of pain, although Casey knew it was really just the hydraulics fighting to keep the legs from buckling.

"Get in the van!" the girl ordered the Reapers, shoving the four boys inside the waiting vehicle. Then she ran over to Casey and hauled her off the ground. She was surprisingly strong, despite her size. Casey stumbled along beside her, relieved to be out of the firing line.

As soon as they were all in the van, the driver slammed the accelerator, and they tore away down the street. Behind them the injured walking machine stumbled left and right, trying not to fall over.

Casey stared at her diminutive saviour with a mixture of awe and gratitude.

"Who are you?" she asked.

"We're the Resistance," the girl snapped. "But the real question is: who the hell are you guys?"

8
DOLLAR DOLLAR BILLS, Y'ALL

Pete watched Xander dive into the swimming pool, piercing the water like a spear. The YouTuber's body was taut and muscled, the payoff for the endless hours he invested in the mansion's gym. Two girls, wearing matching bikinis and mirrored sunglasses, floated in the middle of the pool on the back of an inflatable unicorn with a rainbow mane. They giggled as Xander burst out of the water beside them. Pete wondered why the girls needed sunglasses indoors. The autumn light that filtered through the steamed-up windows around the pool room was dull and grey.

Beyond the windows, across the landscaped gardens, a couple of Red Caps patrolled the edge of the property. Pete couldn't honestly say that their presence made him feel safer. Sometimes he wondered if they were there to keep the downtrodden, hungry citizens beyond the gates out, or him a captive inside. At least, he thought, his cell was comfortable.

He pulled some grapes from a fruit bowl beside the sunloungers and popped them in his mouth, making sure he savoured each one. Fruit was such a rarity these days, a luxury reserved for those few human collaborators who were in the Red Eyes' favour. He sighed and turned back to his laptop.

One of the girls leaned over and kissed Xander before breaking away and pushing his head under the water. Pete envied the YouTuber his easy charisma. Everyone seemed to fall under his spell. The whole planet was glued to their screens whenever he updated the public on the invaders' latest plans. His larger-than-life personality made him the perfect frontman for the aliens, smoothing the way for their occupation of the Earth as they searched for the psionic array.

Xander swam gracefully under the water and emerged at Pete's feet. He rested his elbows on the edge of the pool and stared up at his friend. "Why don't you join us?"

"I've got to write a report about the last piece of the array," Pete said, indicating his laptop.

"The Red Eyes will be busy examining the latest piece of the puzzle for a couple of weeks yet. You can afford to relax a bit. Have some fun."

"Maybe another time," Pete said, popping another

grape in his mouth. "I'm not a big fan of the water."

Xander ran a hand through his wet hair, slicking it back. "Like I always tell you, kid. The sooner we give them what they want, the sooner we stop being useful to them. We have to string it out. Enjoy all this while it lasts, because who knows what tomorrow will bring…" He pushed off from the side, flashing Pete his trademark "X" with his forefingers, before sinking back under the water.

Pete snorted, annoyed by the YouTuber's failure to take anything seriously. He'd been joined at the hip with Xander ever since they returned to Earth, living with him in this lavish mansion at the Arcturians' indulgence. He'd learned that what you saw with Xander was what you got. He was a strutting peacock who would do anything for an audience. He had no use for anyone who wasn't useful to him. He hadn't even been home to see his family since his return to Earth. But then, Pete thought grimly, he hadn't exactly been a doting son either…

He snapped his laptop shut and stood up – he needed some air. The girls screamed. Xander had tipped their inflatable over, pushing them both into the water. Pete opened the glass door, pleased to get away from the claustrophobic humidity.

As he crossed the black and white tiles of the

mansion's checkerboard hall, the doorbell rang. The butler, a diminutive old man who had worked for the Royal Family before they were imprisoned by the Arcturians, opened the heavy oak door. Two Red Eye aliens stood outside, flanking a hooded overseer. The alien commander, dressed in a long grey cowl, strode into the hall, signalling the escort to wait on the step. As the door closed, the alien removed its hood to reveal a familiar reptilian face.

"Good morning, Overseer," Pete said, nodding respectfully. He still thought of her as Scratch, the nickname Casey had given her back in the shopping centre all those years ago. He didn't dare call her that, of course. She'd earned her coveted promotion to overseer after the invasion and was now head of the Arcturian intelligence services on Earth. She'd taken personal charge of the search for the array, realizing that the role would make her indispensable to the emperor. It also ensured she was a frequent visitor to the house.

"Peter," Scratch rasped in clipped English. "How are you this morning?"

Even though he spoke to her almost every day, Pete still shuddered to hear the alien talking in his native tongue. It felt like an insult. Not content with invading Earth, the aliens had stolen his language, too. He wondered what the Red Eyes spoke in countries like France or Greece. Had they learned the native languages, or had they only bothered with English? *The language of the world*, his geography teacher used to say. That might be true, Pete thought to himself grimly, but Arcturian was the language of the galaxy.

"Shall we sit?" Scratch asked, striding past Pete and leading him towards the oak-panelled library. Before the invasion the mansion had belonged to the Saudi ambassador in London. Now, like everything else, it belonged to the aliens.

Scratch snapped her reptilian talon at the butler. "Bring *klaart*," she ordered, referring to the customary alien beverage, a thick black sludge with a smell that could make wallpaper peel. Pete's stomach sank. Nobody drank *klaart* alone. It was a social drink, designed to be shared equally among those present while plans were formulated and enemies were outwitted. The fact that it tasted like liquid horse manure was something its creators seemed entirely oblivious to.

"Please ask Xander to join us," Pete told the butler. If nothing else, he thought, getting Xander in here would reduce the amount of *klaart* he'd have to drink.

"No," Scratch said firmly. "His presence won't be necessary."

The butler, knowing who was in charge, bowed low in acquiescence and then exited. Scratch lingered at the big mahogany desk in the centre of the library a moment, her taloned claws flicking over the documents and books on ancient archaeology that were laid out across it.

"How is your research going?"

"Good," Pete replied airily. "I should know the location of the final piece of the array soon. Five, maybe six weeks."

"Hmmm," Scratch said, her tone laced with scepticism. "We are lucky to have your expert knowledge at our disposal."

"I only have the few clues Private Ross gave me," Pete replied, referring to the abducted soldier he'd met on the space station above Hosin. Private Ross, a keen gamer, had been forced to design *SkyWake* for the Red Eyes. In doing so, he discovered that the ancient psionic array the Red Eyes wanted was actually hidden on Earth. He kept the secret for years before sharing it with Pete, giving the boy all the information that the Red Eyes so desperately needed. His knowledge had been valuable enough to secure Pete safe passage back to Earth.

Scratch's face was impossible to read. "What a pity his information was so cryptic," she said flatly.

Not for the first time, Pete sensed that Scratch knew he was stringing her along. Xander's plan – to give the Arcturians the information they needed slowly, so as to remain useful – was inevitably coming to an end. They'd only got away with it for this long because the array's security system was proving difficult to access. Until the Arcturians cracked the codes, they wouldn't be able to do anything with the pieces they'd unearthed.

Scratch took a seat in a leather armchair beside the hearth and rearranged the folds of her cowl. A fire crackled in the grate, taking the autumn chill off the oversized room.

"I come with news," the alien announced once she was sitting comfortably. "News about your sister." Pete jolted and he struggled to hide his emotions as he sank into the chair opposite the alien.

"What news?" He desperately wanted to know what had happened to her.

"Last night an unauthorized shuttle made entry and crashed in Hyde Park. We recovered the wreckage and traced it back to Hosin. A few hours later we received reports of a group of teenagers – four boys and a girl – out after curfew."

"And you think it's Casey?" Pete asked. His mind raced. His sister was alive. After all these years, she'd finally come back. A wave of relief washed over him, but also something else he couldn't quite put his finger on. Shame, perhaps?

"The group was tracked to an address in South

London, your parental home. Red Caps were despatched and Goliath support was called in. However, the subjects escaped with the help of a third party."

"What third party?"

"We believe it was the Resistance."

"You're saying my sister is back on Earth and is working with the Resistance?" Pete cried, jumping out of his chair. "Do we know where she is? I need to see her!"

Scratch stared at him a moment. Her thin lizard lips pursed sourly with displeasure. "Her whereabouts are currently unknown. But our forces are combing the area. It won't be long before she's discovered."

"So old Casey's back from the dead, is she?" Xander asked, appearing in the doorway unannounced. He wore a fluffy white robe and dried his hair with a towel. Both were monogrammed with a golden X. "Pretty embarrassing for you, I guess, Overseer," he said, looking at Scratch. "Whatever will the emperor say?"

The alien hissed, her forked tongue appearing and then vanishing between her lips. She'd never had much love for the YouTuber. He was simply a necessary evil, useful only for selling the invaders' propaganda to the public.

"What'll happen when you find her?" Pete asked, sitting back down and trying to keep his voice even.

He thought back to the murderous duel that Casey and Scratch had fought in the Crucible on the space station. He couldn't bear to witness something as terrifying as that again.

Scratch clacked her talons impatiently. "That is still to be decided. First we need to know why she's here and what she intends to do. The data we recovered from the shuttle suggests she was delayed on her trip back to Earth due to a navigational malfunction."

Pete had always hoped against hope that his sister was still alive, perhaps marooned on Hosin. Now he knew she was back on Earth, he felt uneasy. She would see everything he'd done over the last few years. He knew she'd be angry and jump to conclusions, just like she always did. But the truth was, she didn't know what it had been like to watch the Arcturians take over the planet.

"Big sis is gonna rip you a new one," Xander grinned, clapping Pete on the shoulder. "Are you ready for that, kid?" Not for the first time Pete wished his friend would stop calling him kid. He was fifteen now, for goodness' sake.

The butler reappeared carrying a silver tray bearing a tall metal pot of alien design. It was the customary vessel for serving *klaart*. Pete's heart sank when he saw there were only two cups.

Xander flopped into an armchair, sitting sideways in it like he was on a photo shoot for a fashion magazine. His legs dangled over the armrest. Scratch stared at him in disgust.

"Your feet," Pete whispered. "You need to cover them up."

"Huh?" Xander grunted, looking down at his open-toe slippers.

"It's a big no-no in Arcturian culture to show bare feet. They consider it rude. Don't you pay any attention?"

Xander let out a mirthless snort. "Why should I when I've got my own personal expert to correct me? We'll have to get you an honorary degree in extraterrestrial cultural relations or something…" He rolled his eyes and covered his feet with the towel. "Better?"

Scratch ignored him and poured out the *klaart*, letting the steaming hot sludge fill the two cups. She passed one to Pete. "*Tarch re hal*," she said.

"*Hal re tarch*," the boy replied, bowing over the cup in the standard acknowledgement. It was like saying "cheers". The only difference was if you failed to say "cheers" back to someone in English, you didn't run the risk of being forced into a fight to the death. Arcturian culture was like that. The slightest hint of an insult always led to some form of combat.

The alien sipped her *klaart*, savouring it. "There is

another matter we need to talk about."

Xander spoke before Pete could respond. "Our next broadcast, right? I've got some ideas about changing the camera angles, adding some new graphics, mixing things up a bit. We've got to keep the audience engaged, right? Huh, what am I saying? You don't know anything about the media side of things. That's why you need me."

Scratch blinked sideways, like a lizard. Pete was accustomed to the differences in the Arcturians' anatomy. He'd even come to admire their reptilian skin, in particular the way that each had a different pattern on their scales. They were all distinct, once you knew what to look for. It was quite beautiful, really.

"We need to talk about the final piece of the array," the alien said, ignoring Xander and addressing Pete directly in Arcturian. "Now that your sister has returned, I need you to expedite the discovery of its location. I can't allow her to delay our plans."

"What's she saying?" Xander asked with a frown. He'd never made any effort to learn Arcturian. Pete pretended to sip his *klaart*, wondering why the alien wanted to keep the YouTuber out of the loop. Whatever the reason, he quite liked the feeling of power it gave him. After spending four years in the YouTuber's shadow, it made a pleasant change.

Lisa, one of the girls from the pool, appeared in the doorway. She was still in her bikini and carelessly left a trail of wet footprints in her wake. A maid hurried behind her with a cloth, trying to mop up the water before it spoiled the expensive oak flooring. Scratch shuddered at the sight of the girl's naked feet.

"Xander," Lisa purred, as if the alien wasn't even there, "can we go for a ride on your motorbike now? You promised, remember?"

Xander nodded and stood up. "Duty calls," he smirked. "We still need to talk about the next broadcast, though. The production values need a major overhaul. Better lighting, cleaner camerawork, and we need to fire that new producer, too. She doesn't have a clue what she's doing. If you want me on-screen addressing the whole planet, we can't make it look like *The Great British Bake Off*. We need to have some class. Do it properly. It's for the win."

With that, he headed over to the door. Before he departed, he turned back to look at Pete. "Don't go native on me, now," he warned his friend, with a winning grin. "First you learn Arcturian, then you drink *klaart*. Before you know it, you'll be covered in scales and forcing me to fight you to the death." He laughed and draped his arm around Lisa's wet shoulders. "C'mon, babe. This conversation was boring, anyway."

Scratch sipped her *klaart*, waiting until they were gone. She looked at Pete over the rim of her cup.

"That boy is rude, disrespectful and a total liability."

Pete shrugged. "But you need him."

"Do I? I think it might be time to terminate his services. After all, the array is almost ours."

Pete swallowed again. "And when you have it, will you terminate my services too?"

Scratch set her cup down. "That depends how useful you can be to us, Peter. I've been willing to let you stall for time up until now, since it allowed me to consolidate my position here on Earth. But now that your sister has returned…"

"You want to hurry up and activate the array before she can stop you?"

Scratch nodded tightly.

"You'll need to crack the access codes," Pete said, thinking about the layer of security the Squids had used to protect the array's systems. He didn't know much about it except that it was very hard to break.

"I'm told our technical team is very close."

Pete thought a moment, trying to play all the angles like Xander had taught him. "If I manage to tell you where the piece of the puzzle is ahead of schedule, I'd like something in return."

"You want me to guarantee your sister's safety?"

Scratch guessed, her black eyes dancing with scorn. "You humans are so predictable."

Pete paused and sipped his bitter *klaart*.

"No, I want you to guarantee *mine*…"

Scratch baulked in surprise. Then a hideous smile, full of malice, flashed across her face.

"It seems Xander has taught you well."

Pete felt his stomach churn. He wasn't sure if it was the foul-smelling alien drink, or a feeling of utter shame.

9

THE RESISTANCE NEEDS YOU!

The first thing Casey recognized was the smell. A vague aroma of stale sweat and kebab meat that made her nose twitch, kindling a long-forgotten memory in the depths of her mind. The Resistance had parked their grubby van under a railway arch in a rundown part of the city before leading Casey and her friends through an alleyway into a dilapidated building. As soon as Casey entered, the odour hit her. Her suspicions were confirmed when she saw the rows of arcade cabinets, now all switched off, stretching through the gloom.

"FunZone?" she whispered. "Your base is in FunZone?"

"You know this place?" asked the petite girl who had rescued them from the walking machine.

"I came here once, a long time ago," Casey replied. "I thought they'd demolished it and turned it into flats." She looked around the cavernous arcade, recalling how her dad had bought his *Space Invaders* machine here years before. The windows at the front of the arcade had since been boarded up, leaving it even darker and dingier than Casey remembered, but there was no mistaking the arcade's stagnant smell.

"We found it a couple of months ago after our last place got raided," the girl explained. "We've got beds upstairs and we're trying to connect up some solar panels so we can get the power on again. It's not exactly five-star luxury, but it'll do."

She led them through the rows of lifeless arcade machines, ignoring the excited chatter of the boys. Elite and Cheeze paused a moment to stick their heads inside a sit-down *Jurassic Park* game. Before they could reach for the plastic light guns inside it, a stern look from the girl hurried them along.

"This is our armoury," she said, waving towards a workbench where a group of teens sorted through scavenged weapons. With the exception of a couple of plasma pistols, most of the pile was low-tech – some gardening tools, a rusty ceremonial sword and an old musket that looked like it had been found in an antique shop. The teens at the workbench looked up as the gamers passed. Their faces were sallow and undernourished, and their eyes were full of suspicion.

They wore black beanies and fingerless gloves in an attempt to keep out the chill. Without any electricity, the air was brittle with cold.

"You guys are the Resistance?" Casey asked.

"Just what's left of it. No weapons, not much food, and dwindling numbers. But we're still fighting." She extended a small hand to Casey. "I'm Jude, by the way."

"Casey."

"I saw what you did back there," Jude continued, examining Casey like she was some kind of human puzzle. "Lifting those cars into the air. Throwing them across the street. Not sure how you did it, but it was incredible."

"I'm not sure how I did it either, to be honest," Casey admitted.

The girl stared at her quizzically a moment, then decided not to press the issue. "Are you guys hungry?" she asked. "We don't have much, but you're welcome to share it." She led them to a table where there were some ration packs along with a stale hunk of bread and a sweaty piece of cheese that looked like it had been out of the fridge for too long.

Fish grabbed a yellow tube of nutritional paste from a ration pack and squeezed some onto his finger. "Hey, it's vanilla flavoured," he said, surprised. He took another lick. "It's better than that tasteless muck they served us on the command platform."

A huge map of the city was pinned on the wall nearby. While the others sampled the food, Casey and Brain examined it. London had been divided up into sectors by the aliens. Red crosses on the map marked various checkpoints, and a building in the East End was circled in marker pen. Someone had scribbled the words *Main Supply Warehouse* alongside it.

"That map's out of date," a boy said, coming up beside them. Casey recognized him from the checkpoint. He was big and broad with a weightlifter's bulky arms and a Nigerian accent. "We just don't have the manpower to keep track of the invaders' movements any more. I'm Babatunde. We ran into one another on the bridge earlier. In fact, I think we almost ran you over." His deep laugh boomed around the echoey arcade, full of friendly camaraderie.

"Baba was one of the first Resistance fighters," Jude explained. "He worked out how to reprogram the drones and he's been turning them against the aliens ever since."

"Four years of hacking their tech," Babatunde said, "and they still haven't worked out how to stop me."

"You should talk to Cheeze, bruv," Elite told him. "He's our tech whizz."

Babatunde's eyes rested on Cheeze's hoverchair and he let out an impressed whistle. "You built that yourself?

You're going to have to let me take a look under the hood."

"Only if you show me how you've been reprogramming the drones," Cheeze replied. "The attack algorithm you used on the bridge was really something. You didn't lose a single machine."

While the boys chatted, Casey took another look at the map. Seeing her home city carved up by the invaders felt like an affront. What right did these aliens have to mess with London?

"Aren't any adults fighting back?" she asked Jude, glancing around at the teenage Resistance members.

"Lots of them did at the beginning," the girl explained. "My parents ran raids against the Red Eyes in the early days. They were chemistry teachers and they used to make their own explosives. They even took out an Arcturian troop carrier once. There are still a few adults helping us, but most people are too scared of reprisals. The Red Caps keep everyone in a constant state of fear. The Arcturians recruited all the bullies and sadists and put them in uniforms."

Casey thought of her mum working at the hospital, trying to help people, resisting in her own way. "Are your parents still fighting?"

Jude shook her head. "They were rounded up a year ago. The Red Eyes gave them a choice: join the excavation teams or face the death penalty. They're still out there somewhere, digging in the dirt and looking for whatever it is the Arcturians are turning the world upside down for."

"I'm sorry," Casey whispered. "They must be proud of you for continuing the fight, though."

"I guess," Jude said, staring into the distance. "Sometimes I think I'm just as stupid as they were. I mean, this isn't a battle we're going to win." She shrugged away her gloom. "But what else are we going to do, right? Go and play *Blocka* all day?"

There was a thud and a door in the boards covering the front of the arcade opened. A thin shaft of moonlight fell through it as two boys stumbled inside. One of them, an Asian teenager with jet black hair, clutched his side. Blood seeped between his fingers.

"Haruto!" Jude cried, running over. She put her head out of the door to check no one was watching and then shut it quickly behind them. "What happened?"

"We got ambushed by a patrol at the train station," explained the other boy, who looked about the same age. "They're everywhere tonight."

"Bring him over here," ordered a tall redheaded girl, pointing to the snooker tables at the back of the arcade. She opened up a med kit and pulled out supplies. Fish stared at her in wonder. She was the girl he'd seen at the checkpoint.

The Resistance fighters helped the boy called Haruto over to one of the snooker tables and lifted him onto the green baize. Casey sensed it wasn't the first time it had been used as a makeshift operating table. He groaned in pain as he lay back.

"How bad is it, Marguerite?" Jude asked.

The redhead snapped on a pair of latex gloves before cutting away Haruto's tactical vest and T-shirt to expose the wound. There was a deep gouge in the boy's side, just above his hip bone. She examined it with confident, nimble fingers, ignoring his grunts of pain. "He'll live," she said. "But he's gonna get a cool scar to impress the girls with."

Haruto didn't crack a smile. He was too busy frowning at the Reapers. "Who are they?" he demanded. "You know the rules: no strangers."

"We rescued them while you were out," Jude explained. "They got into a tussle with a Goliath. Held their own pretty well, even though they didn't have weapons."

"They fought a Goliath unarmed?" Haruto asked, disbelieving. He grunted in pain as Marguerite washed out his wound.

Jude took out her phone. "I caught it all on video," she explained, showing him a clip of Casey throwing the parked cars at the Goliath. "See why I brought them here?"

"How the hell did you do that?" Haruto asked sharply, looking up at Casey. "Is it some kind of trick? CGI?"

Casey wasn't sure how to explain everything that had happened to her on Hosin. Did the Resistance even know who the Squids were, or about their telepathic powers? She guessed they hadn't been *SkyWake* players, and she wasn't sure they'd believe her if she told them the truth.

"No trick, bruv," Elite interrupted. "My girl here's got mad powers. You ain't seen nothing. She's gonna bring the pain to the Red Eyes."

"And we're gonna help," Fish added, making sure Marguerite was listening. "We hate the Red Eyes just as much as you guys. They've abducted us, shot at us, blown us up, sent robot spiders after us, imprisoned us and killed our friends. We can help you. *She* can help you."

Haruto regarded Casey warily for a moment.

"We don't need your help," he told her.

Then he slumped back on the snooker table and passed out.

10

HADOUKEN!

Over the following week, while Haruto recuperated, Casey and her teammates stayed with the Resistance. Jude set up camp beds for them in the room above the arcade and it wasn't long before they felt like they were part of the group. Despite their fierce appearance, the Resistance fighters proved welcoming and friendly. They were keen to hear the Reapers' stories about what had happened to them in space. In exchange, they told their own tales about the Arcturian invasion.

On the first night, as they huddled together to keep warm in the chilly arcade, the Reapers listened in awed silence as Jude talked. She told them how the Resistance movement had grown from its early beginnings, and the sacrifices that so many had made to fight back against the aliens. After hearing what had happened to these teenagers' parents – who'd been imprisoned or worse by the Arcturians – the boys decided to wait a few days longer before trying to contact their own families.

Haruto was the leader of the group and Jude seemed to be his unofficial second in command. She was quieter and, Casey thought, smarter, too. The Asian boy, giving orders from his sick bed upstairs, was a brilliant tactician, but he could be quick to anger. When his spikiness offended, Jude stepped in and effortlessly smoothed things over. She had an easy way of making people feel valued, and she kept the group's spirits up amid the hardship.

The biggest problems the Resistance faced were dwindling numbers and dwindling supplies. In the early days of the invasion, Jude explained, there'd been a much bigger network of people willing to take up arms against the invaders. The Resistance had sprung up in cities across the world, a self-organizing movement united by a shared desire: freedom. There had been cells in all the major cities led by former soldiers, police officers, paramedics, construction workers and shop assistants. Ordinary people doing extraordinary things. One of the most famous was a Year Six teacher in Newcastle, who had proved to be a daring guerrilla commander. She was as much surprised by this turn of events as anyone.

The Resistance honed their skills in the streets,

launching raids against the enemy in an attempt to wear them down. But the more they tried to recruit new members, the more spies the Red Eyes set upon them.

"The Resistance was caught in a bind," Jude told Casey one morning over breakfast. "If we'd just been fighting against the aliens, it would have been easy to tell who the enemy was. But the minute people started collaborating with the lizards, the lines between the two sides were blurred. We were betrayed over and over again. No matter how hard we tried, our cells kept getting busted. People would be captured and spill their guts. Or they'd sell out their comrades for a few luxuries."

"How could they betray their friends like that?" Casey asked, shocked.

"It happens," Jude shrugged. "Nobody thinks they'd ever do it until they get captured."

"Well, I never would," Casey said. "And neither would my teammates." She couldn't think of anything worse than collaborating with the enemy. The thought inevitably stirred up memories of her brother's betrayal. She felt the bile rising in her chest. She wasn't sure she could ever forgive him for what he'd done. She decided not to mention him to Jude. Mostly, she realized, because she was embarrassed.

Although Haruto had rejected the Reapers' help,

Jude was keen to learn everything she could from the new arrivals. She was particularly interested in the time Casey had spent on Hosin. She listened with rapt attention as Casey told her about the war on the planet, her meeting with the Squids, and what Xolotl had said would happen if the Arcturians managed to activate the psionic array. Casey explained that the Squids had built the device to communicate across the galaxy telepathically. But in the wrong hands, it could be used as a weapon to enslave others.

"So, this isn't just a battle for Earth," Jude murmured when Casey was finished. "It's bigger than that, isn't it?"

"We're fighting to stop the Red Eyes taking over the whole galaxy," Casey said. "That's why we need your help."

Jude looked defeated. "I'm not sure there's enough of us," she whispered. "We're not an army. Not any more."

Over the next few days, in an attempt to earn their keep, the Reapers helped Babatunde with the solar panels. He'd scavenged them from abandoned buildings across the city, carting them through the streets late at night to avoid Red Cap patrols. When he'd found enough, he mounted them on the flat roof at the rear of FunZone. It was south facing and perfectly positioned to catch the sun's rays. Yet, try as he might, he couldn't get the panels to generate electricity.

"I'm a coder not an engineer," he explained as he showed them the rooftop set-up one morning. "I just don't know how to do it."

"Can't you just watch a YouTube video?" Fish suggested helpfully. "That's how I learn to do everything. Cook an egg, finish all the side quests in *Zelda*, survive avalanches…"

Babatunde shook his head. "YouTube's gone. Plus TikTok and Insta and Snapchat, and even Wikipedia. The Red Eyes censored the whole Internet. The only thing you can do online is play *Blocka*."

"What about getting a book on solar power, then?"

"The Red Caps shut all the libraries and bookshops."

"They banned *books*?" Elite cried. "What are they? Space Nazis?"

"It's worse than that," Babatunde sighed. "They told people they could use them for firewood."

As they chatted, Brain examined the bundle of cables attached to the solar panels.

"It looks like the problem is the inverter."

"Really?" Babatunde asked. "What's wrong with it?"

Brain pushed his glasses up his nose. "Well, strictly speaking what's wrong with the inverter is that there isn't an inverter. You need one to change the direct current the panels produce into alternating current to power the building."

"AC/DC," Cheeze agreed. "That's the issue."

"AC/DC?" Fish asked, struggling to keep up with the tech talk. "You mean like the rock band?" He played air guitar, ignoring Brain's impatient scowl.

It took two days of careful scavenging before they found a suitable inverter in an abandoned house in East Dulwich. Working with Brain and Cheeze, Babatunde wired it up to the solar panels. When it was finally ready, the teenagers from the Resistance gathered around the fuse box to watch, excited that they might finally get heating in the draughty arcade.

"Let there be light!" Babatunde boomed and, with a theatrical flourish, he switched the generator on. Nothing happened and, for a moment, Casey thought their efforts had been in vain. Then there was a sudden hum as every arcade cabinet in the place came on. The screens lit up as the circuit boards cycled through their boot sequences. A minute later, the arcade erupted in a cacophony of bleeps and bloops. Casey felt a happy rush of nostalgia. This was the FunZone she remembered.

The Resistance cheered and rushed to try out the machines. Cheeze showed them how to open the cabinets and switch them to free-play mode, which meant you didn't need any coins to play. Pretty soon they were all shooting, jumping and flying through virtual worlds.

Casey just looked on, soaking up the atmosphere. It was the happiest she'd seen the Resistance since she'd arrived. The battle-weary guerrillas were desperate for a break from Red Eye patrols and food worries.

"Great job!" Jude said, coming up beside Casey. "Your friends deserve a medal. Baba's been trying to fix the solar panels for the last month."

"Do you like gaming?" Casey asked, pausing in front of a *Crazy Taxi* machine.

"Not especially," Jude confessed with a shy shrug. "Personally, I'm just relieved we can have the heating on." She blew out a deep breath, watching the cloud of condensation form in the chilly air.

"Hey, Casey! Come and see this," Cheeze called over. "They've got a *Street Fighter II* machine and Brain is a total beast on it."

Casey and Jude headed over to where a bunch of their friends had gathered around a colourful cabinet, watching a battle between Brain and Fish. Brain was playing as Ryu, a muscled martial artist in a white karate suit and a red headband. Fish was Chun-Li, a Chinese girl with an ox horn hairdo and a bright blue dress that flapped as she kicked her powerful legs.

It wasn't a fair fight. Brain was unleashing an unstoppable assault on Fish, his hands moving deftly over the controls, one combo attack following another. Fish didn't know how to counter him. He was getting creamed.

"Give me a chance," Fish complained, hammering the buttons and joystick.

"*Hadouken!*" Ryu shouted on-screen and a ball of blue energy shot out of his hands. It flew across the screen towards Chun-Li, knocking her backwards and slicing her health bar almost in half.

Fish sniffed grumpily. "This is ridiculous," he said. "Nobody can shoot fireballs in real life." He whacked the buttons some more, hoping that some random combination might save him.

"It's not a fireball, it's an energy ball," Brain said, without looking up from the screen.

"Oh, well, that makes all the difference. I totally believe in it now."

"*Hadouken!*" Ryu cried again and another orb flew out of his hands.

"*Ha-dou-ken!*" Fish muttered, mimicking Ryu's voice. "What does it even mean?"

"It's Japanese for *surge fist*," Brain told him. His mouth twitched into a smile as Ryu jumped through the air and delivered a spinning kick that knocked Chun-Li off her feet for good. She crumpled to the floor. The Resistance fighters cheered, impressed.

"No fair!" Fish cried. "How do you even know all these special moves?"

"It's a fighting game, but the most powerful muscle is up here," Brain said, tapping his temple. "You've got to learn the combos, not just mash all the buttons." He waggled the joystick to demonstrate the special attack combination. "The *hadouken* is down, down and forward, forward and punch. It's an art."

Fish was unimpressed.

The redheaded girl smiled at him. "You'll get him next time," she said, patting him on the arm.

Fish blushed, suddenly tongue-tied. "Yeah, er, thanks, um…"

"Marguerite. My name's Marguerite."

"Alastair," Fish said, giving her his real name without even thinking about it. He saw Cheeze staring at him, his eyes bugging out.

"Alastair? Your real name's Alastair?"

"Yeah," the Scottish boy said, prickling slightly. It was the first time any of the Reapers besides Casey had revealed their own names. "What's yours, then?"

A furious voice interrupted them.

"Did the war just end, or have you all lost your minds?" Haruto demanded, standing in the doorway that led to the snooker tables. His skinny chest was bare apart from a thick white surgical bandage that had been wrapped around his ribs. "You're making so much noise every Red Eye in the city probably knows we're here."

An embarrassed silence fell over the crowd. Babatunde flicked the fuse box and the machines fell silent. Gloom quickly descended on FunZone, bringing the Resistance fighters back to their senses.

"Before you turn the power on again, make sure those blasted machines are off," Haruto warned.

"I'm guessing he isn't a gamer," Fish muttered under his breath.

Later, as the electric heaters warmed the vast space, Haruto joined Casey and the Reapers as they ate. He sawed a hunk of bread from a stale loaf, folded it in half and squeezed some nutritional paste onto it. He chewed the makeshift sandwich thoughtfully. Jude and Babatunde sat either side of him.

"How are you feeling?" Casey asked, trying to build bridges.

"Better now it's warm," Haruto said through a mouthful of bread. He took a slurp of water to wash it down. "I hear you helped Baba get the power on," he said, looking at Brain and Cheeze. "Thank you."

"Pleasure," Brain said. He nodded at the Resistance's tech expert. "But Baba did all the hard work. We just helped get it over the line."

Haruto nodded, clearly pleased at their willingness to share the credit. "So," he said, looking across the table to his second in command, "me and Jude have been talking. She thinks we should join forces with you. And if there's one thing I've learned it's that she has good instincts when it comes to picking people."

"See? He's really a big softy under that gruff exterior," Jude laughed, punching Haruto's arm.

The boy grunted in mock pain. "Hey, go easy on me, I'm still injured."

Casey looked at the Reapers, checking they were on board. They nodded.

"We'd definitely be up for joining forces," she told Haruto. "What can we do to help?"

Haruto tossed the remains of his sandwich aside. "We have an informer who knows the location of the final piece of the array. Apparently it's here in the UK. They say it's going to be activated in a few days in the presence of the Arcturian emperor himself."

Casey tensed. She had hoped they would have more time. But maybe this was the break they needed.

"What's the plan?" she asked.

Haruto pushed back in his chair. "I want to assassinate the emperor when he arrives to unveil the array." He looked around the room, clearly anticipating approval at this suggestion.

"*What?*" Brain growled, leaping out of his seat. "That's the most idiotic thing I've ever heard!"

Casey had never seen Brain so annoyed. He was

normally calm and mild-mannered, keeping his emotions under wraps.

Haruto looked taken aback. "If you want to kill a snake, you cut off its head," he said defensively.

"But Arcturian culture isn't like that," Brain continued, exasperated. "If you kill the emperor, someone else will just take their place. They're all about hierarchy and order. Surely you have a better plan than this?"

Brain looked at Jude, but the girl kept her eyes fixed firmly on the table's surface.

The next voice that spoke belonged to Babatunde. "There is another option," he said. "Me and Cheeze have been doing some research. We think we might have a way to stop the Red Eyes from activating the array." He signalled for Cheeze to explain.

The tech wizard cleared his throat. "What do you guys know about this *Blocka* game everyone's playing?"

"It's how the lizards divide up the food rations," Haruto told him. "Everyone has to play it to win points. The more points they get, the more food they earn."

"Well, I took a look at it," Cheeze continued. "It's not exactly fun to play. You just sort and arrange blocks." He tapped his phone and opened the *Blocka* app he'd downloaded onto it.

"Is it like *Tetris*?" Fish asked, looking over Cheeze's shoulder. "I used to love that game. But the crazy

Russian music made it real stressful."

"No," Cheeze continued. "*Tetris* was fun. This is more like a scientific discovery game."

"Again, bruv," Elite interrupted. "But in English this time."

"*Blocka* isn't really a game. It's a way to crunch data. Sometimes, when scientists have loads of information to analyse, they turn it into a game and get ordinary people to play it. Whenever someone plays, they're actually helping the scientists analyse the data and—"

Elite held a hand in the air, stopping Cheeze in mid-flow. "I said *in English*, bruv."

"It's called crowdsourcing," Brain said. "You get lots of people to help you analyse a big pool of data. There used to be an online puzzle game like this where you designed molecules for RNA-based medicines and—"

Elite groaned. "Am I the only one who's not following all this geek speak?" He looked at Fish for support but his friend just shrugged.

Casey interrupted. "What you're saying is that *Blocka* is actually a tool? The Red Eyes have got billions of people all over the world sorting data for them every day? Why?"

"We think it's got something to do with the array," Babatunde explained.

Cheeze nodded. "When the Squids built this thing,

they added a security system to it to prevent it being activated by accident. The Red Eyes are trying to crack the code so they can fire up the device as soon as they've found all the pieces."

Brain's eyes lit up. "If we took the *Blocka* servers offline, no one would be able to play the game any more. We could stop the Red Eyes from cracking the array's security. The device would be useless!"

"Exactly!" Cheeze grinned. "Me and Baba think we can hack their hack."

Haruto had had enough. "This is all just guesswork," he complained. "We could be wasting our time." He looked at Cheeze disdainfully. "Who even are you? Some schoolboy hacker?"

"No," Casey said firmly. "He's the only hacker who's ever worked with the Squids. If anyone knows what they're talking about, it's Cheeze."

"There's just one problem," Babatunde said. "In order to take down the servers we'll need to attack the main data centre in the city."

"That's suicide!" Haruto cried. "It's surrounded by Red Eyes."

"We could do it," Jude interjected. "If we had proper weapons." She pointed to the map on the wall. "We know the main supply depot for the city is in the East End of London, on the Isle of Dogs."

"So, let's get over there, bruv," Elite said, banging the table with his fist.

"It's not that easy," Babatunde explained. "Only Red Cap commanders can access the depot's inventory, and the whole system is automated. The commander tells the warehouse what he needs. It gets loaded onto a truck by drones and delivered wherever he wants. But before you can start the process, you need a commander's access card. Believe it or not, we don't have any Red Cap commanders on our friends list."

A slow smile crept over Casey's face. "What if I told you I knew a commander who was friendly? A little too friendly, actually…"

Haruto sat up straighter in his chair, suddenly intrigued.

"Can you get him to help us?"

"I think so." Casey smiled. "But first I need to find my mum a new cocktail dress."

11

ARMY OF THE SHADOWS

The team left FunZone when it was dark. Seven days had passed since they had been rescued by the Resistance and the authorities' search for them had fizzled out. Clouds hung heavy in the black sky as they stepped out of the arcade, blotting out the stars, the autumn moon and even the Red Eyes' space station that rotated above the planet. All the better, Casey thought, given the stealth mission they were about to embark upon.

Haruto drove the Luton van, the one with CLEAN ME! scrawled along its grimy side. Jude rode shotgun. The cargo area was stacked from floor to ceiling with cardboard boxes marked: BAKED GOODS. Casey and the Reapers had created a secret hiding place among the boxes and they hid there with Babatunde and Marguerite. It was cramped and uncomfortable, and it reminded Casey of the simple dirt houses she built in

Minecraft – the ones that would help you get through your first night in survival mode without being mobbed by creepers and zombies.

The van rolled through the dark streets for an hour before Casey felt it slow down. At first she thought they'd reached their destination and she looked forward to being able to stretch her legs. A sharp warning from Haruto made her realize this was just wishful thinking.

"Checkpoint ahead," the Resistance leader said through the small viewing hatch between the cab and the cargo area. "Keep your heads down."

The van stopped in front of a huge metal checkpoint that blocked the road. A Goliath stood to the side, its huge chassis silhouetted in the gloom. Haruto and Jude shielded their eyes from the glare as the Red Caps manning the checkpoint swung a floodlight towards them. Two soldiers approached the van with slow, heavy footsteps. Both carried plasma rifles.

Haruto wound down his window.

"ID cards," the first Red Cap barked, his voice sharp.

Hiding in the back of the van, Casey listened to the conversation with bated breath. She wondered why anyone would choose to work for the Arcturians. Jude had said that most of the Red Caps were bullies, but Casey guessed some people did it out of necessity. Being a soldier was one of the few jobs that guaranteed you'd get a ration pack without having to compete for points playing *Blocka*.

"Where are you going?" the second Red Cap asked, less aggressive than her colleague.

"We're delivering food to the commanders in Sector B," Haruto explained, gesturing to the back of the vehicle. Casey's heart beat a little faster. If the Red Caps decided to search the cargo bay, they'd be caught. She didn't fancy their chances of getting away with a Goliath standing right over them.

"Food? What kind of food?" the man demanded.

"Just some baked goods." There was an edge in Haruto's voice that sounded a little too defensive to Casey's ears. A torch flashed inside the cab, casting shadows on the roof of the cargo bay through the hatch. Casey and the others froze in the dark watching the patterns created by the light.

"Get out slowly and open up the back of the vehicle," the female soldier instructed.

"Yes, officer," Jude replied meekly. Casey listened as two pairs of footsteps headed to the rear of the van. Beside her, Elite tensed. Casey squeezed his arm and put a finger to her lips, warning him not to move. She knew he hated small spaces like this, but if he freaked out now they'd be dead for sure. Cheeze, sitting in his deactivated hoverchair, stared at the floor nervously. He probably felt more vulnerable than any of them.

There was a loud clatter as the shutter at the back of the van rolled up. The Red Cap's torch flashed into the cargo bay, illuminating the stacks of boxes. From the outside, the cargo bay looked completely full. You'd have to remove three whole rows of boxes to discover the hidden space where Casey and her friends hid, holding their breath.

"Where's all this going?" the female Red Cap asked Jude, her voice muffled by the boxes that separated her from the Reapers.

"Big party happening in Sector B tomorrow," the girl explained. There was a sliver of dissatisfaction in her voice, as if she didn't approve of such things.

The Red Cap grunted. "Well, I'll need to check your inventory."

Casey peered through the hatch into the cab. Haruto, still behind the wheel, slowly took a plasma pistol from under the driver's seat. He held it, hidden, in his lap. She prayed he wouldn't be rash.

"How many boxes are in here?" the Red Cap asked.

"One hundred and fifty-four," Jude replied. "But there's only a hundred and fifty on the manifest. Can you believe it? They've got so much food that they're not even keeping track of it properly. Muffins, doughnuts, croissants, we're like a sugar rush on wheels."

"Commanders always eat well," the woman agreed bitterly. "I can't remember the last time I had a muffin." She sighed. "You're going to have to unload it all so we can check it. Sorry, it's just the way it is."

"OK, I understand."

Casey heard the petite girl remove the first couple of boxes and place them on the ground. "You know," Jude said, chatting away as she worked, "what gets me is that the commanders get all the rewards without doing any of the hard work. I mean, you don't see them out here in the dead of night, do you?"

The Red Cap snorted, amused by the girl's world-weary attitude. "No, you don't."

"How long's your shift?" Jude continued.

"We're here until breakfast."

"Pretty cold."

"Always is."

Jude lifted another box out of the van. "We've still got another hour's drive to go. Last time we arrived a couple of minutes late and they docked our rations." She paused a moment. "It's going to take me a good half-hour to unload all of this and the same again to put it all back. Do you think there's another way we can solve this?"

"What are you suggesting?" the Red Cap asked. It felt like they were dancing around one another, neither wanting to say too much.

"Well," Jude mumbled, "if you didn't need to check the manifest too closely, those extra boxes could maybe get lost in transit. A few pastries might take the chill off. A couple of boxes for you guys, a couple for me and the driver…"

There was a long pause. Casey strained to hear what was happening. She wondered if Jude had misjudged it.

"Lock her up!" the female Red Cap ordered.

Casey froze. *Was the soldier talking about Jude?*

Elite looked as if he was about to burst through the wall of boxes in panic. Babatunde squeezed his arm to reassure him. Casey waited a moment, straining to hear what was going on outside. Fish and Marguerite stared at one another in horror.

There was a sudden clang as the van's rear shutter was pulled down and locked into place. Casey sighed with relief.

The soldier was talking about locking up the VAN!

"She's good to go!" the female Red Cap called out, banging the side of the vehicle with her fist. Jude climbed into the passenger seat as the engine started up. A moment later the vehicle rolled through the checkpoint under the legs of the Goliath.

Through the viewing hatch Casey caught a quick glimpse of the Red Caps as they ripped open their boxes of baked goods.

"We're safe, guys!" Jude called through to the back, giddy with relief. "Never underestimate the power of a double chocolate chip muffin!"

The van escaped the city centre without any more stops, chugging through the suburban streets. There was no other traffic and the endless rows of houses were silent and still, curtains drawn. It was like driving through a ghost town.

"Where is everyone?" Casey whispered, watching through the hatch.

"People are too scared to be seen outside," Haruto murmured. "It's been like this since the Betrayal. People prefer to stay hidden, keeping their heads down. As soon as the government sold out, we knew it was everyone for themselves."

"The Betrayal?" Casey asked.

"What else would you call it when every government and every corporation in the world decides to work with alien invaders instead of protecting their people?" He stared straight ahead, his hands gripping the steering wheel tightly.

"I'm sorry," Casey said and, without thinking, she reached a hand through the hatch to touch his shoulder. As she did, a burst of light exploded inside her head. She had a sudden vision of Haruto, years earlier, running along a street with his parents. Red Eye attack ships flew overhead, firing indiscriminately at a crowd of fleeing civilians. Casey felt his panic as explosions rocked the street. A second later, his parents vanished in a burst of plasma.

Casey's body convulsed with shock and grief at the vision. This was why he was so angry, she realized. Her hand tightened on the boy's shoulder.

"What are you doing?" Haruto asked, taking his eyes off the road to glare at her. "Trying to break my bones?"

"Sorry, I don't know my own strength," Casey mumbled. She sat down on the floor of the cargo bay, trembling. Somehow she'd felt his thoughts as if they were her own. She remembered the Squids' ability to step into her mind at will. It seemed she'd discovered this power too.

She saw Cheeze staring at her, concerned. He always seemed to know when something was wrong.

"I'm fine," she muttered before he could say anything. She thought about telling him what had just happened. But something stopped her. Haruto's vision felt private, something she'd stumbled across uninvited. It wasn't hers to share. She rested her back against the boxes and sighed. The Resistance leader's anger had shaken her.

The van slowed, jolting her out of her thoughts.

"This is the place," Jude called back to them,

pointing over to an industrial estate. A man in a trench coat stood on the street corner, holding a storm lantern.

"Is that the signal?" Haruto asked.

Jude peered out of the windscreen. "They said he'd be carrying a torch."

"Well, that's not a torch…"

"Maybe it's not him. Be careful."

The van rolled to a stop beside the man. Haruto wound down his window.

"Hey," he said, one hand on the steering wheel while the other gripped the plasma pistol hidden in his lap.

"Hey," the man replied. He was unshaven and had darting, nervous eyes.

"Don't you have a proper torch?" Haruto asked.

The man ignored him. "The moon's behind the clouds tonight," he muttered and then waited expectantly for a reply.

"But better weather is coming," Jude put in from across the cab.

The man lifted the lantern so he could see her face. "Not soon enough," he said. Then, satisfied with her answer, he added: "Head on through. Fourth building on the right. They're expecting you."

Haruto nodded tersely and gunned the van into the industrial estate. The huge warehouses were quiet and still.

"Who are we meeting?" Brain asked from the cargo bay.

"People who can help us," Haruto said, his eyes constantly scanning the area for any potential ambush.

"Resistance people?" Brain asked.

"Sympathizers."

"Can we trust them?"

"Best not to trust anyone in this line of work," Jude said with a grim finality that made Brain purse his lips and fall silent.

The van pulled up outside a warehouse. Several people carriers sat in the car park and about twenty men and women stood beside them, in the process of changing out of their regular clothes and pulling on kitchen whites. None of them paid any attention as the Reapers climbed out of the back of the Luton van.

"You're late," a bald man with a hint of a French accent said to Haruto.

"We got held up at a checkpoint."

"Trouble?" the Frenchman replied, concerned.

Haruto snorted. "Not this time."

The man rubbed a hand over his hairless head. "It is all very dangerous," he complained. Then he noticed Casey and the Reapers. "I am Marcel," he told them. "I have something for you." He led them to one of the people carriers. Jude, Babatunde and Marguerite followed. Inside were neatly pressed waiters' uniforms all wrapped in plastic. They smelled of dry cleaning. "You're going to be on waiting duty at the reception," he told the group. "Try and find something that fits."

They all dived in, checking out the sizes. Marcel turned to Casey and gestured to the streak of blue in her long hair. "You'll need to tie that back," he told her. "Our Arcturian overlords aren't big fans of finding hair in their *klaart*."

"We used to wear hairnets in my dad's fish 'n' chip shop," Fish said.

"You won't be in the kitchens," the man told him. "You'll be serving drinks and canapés."

As they picked out their uniforms, Casey noticed that Haruto wasn't with them. She looked out of the warehouse door and saw him jogging across the industrial estate, keeping to the shadows. He clutched his side as he went, still recovering from his recent injury.

"Where's he going?" she asked Jude.

"Don't tell anyone, but he's meeting our informer," she replied in a low whisper.

Casey raised her eyebrows, intrigued. "Do you know who they are?" She guessed they must be human. No Arcturian would ever switch sides. Their code of honour stopped them from betraying one another.

Perhaps humans could learn something from it, she thought.

Jude shrugged. "Only Haruto knows, and he won't tell anyone. We've been betrayed so many times." She looked around at the rail of clothes and tutted. "I'd better grab something quickly," she said. "The small sizes always seem to vanish first."

Casey waited until her new friend was occupied, then snuck between the people carriers and followed Haruto as he headed deeper into the industrial estate. She hugged the sides of the warehouses as best she could, slinking along like a cat on the prowl. She'd have given anything for an infiltrator suit like she'd had on the space station above Hosin. At least the lack of streetlights meant there was plenty of darkness to hide in.

Somewhere in the distance an exhaust pipe roared throatily. A single beam of light appeared, cutting through the gloom. She saw Haruto shield his eyes as the headlight of a sleek motorbike dazzled him. A motorcyclist, wearing a black leather motorbike suit and a helmet, pulled up on it. They kept the engine idling, ready to make a quick getaway. In the darkness, Casey couldn't tell whether the rider was male or female. She watched as they handed Haruto a paper file.

"You're sure the location is correct?" Haruto asked. "The emperor will be there?"

The motorcyclist's helmet bobbed an affirmative. They said something Casey couldn't catch.

"I know it's dangerous," Haruto said. "But what else can we do?"

Casey moved forward. As she did, her foot kicked an abandoned beer can. It clattered across the tarmac. Without hesitating, the motorcyclist gunned the bike and raced away. Within seconds, they had vanished into the night.

Haruto spun around.

"You spying on me?" he demanded, seeing Casey.

"Who was that?"

"Someone with information," Haruto said. He tucked the file inside his jacket. "Thanks to them, I know where the final piece of the array is. If your plan fails, I'm going after the emperor."

12

R.S.V.P.

Pete couldn't help but roll his eyes at his official title, Chief Technical Officer. Having only just turned fifteen, he couldn't really take it seriously. He wasn't a chief technical officer, or any other kind of expert. He was just a kid who knew the locations of the various pieces of the array and was trying his best not to get vaporized by aliens.

The title had come out of one of Xander's endless negotiations with Scratch, a throwaway addition to the deal the YouTuber had made. Xander approached negotiating like a general approaches war. He insisted on a contract for everything and pored over every clause, adding in riders and requests wherever he could. Before you knew it he wanted a mansion; a sports car; motorbikes; and an endless supply of Doritos and Mountain Dew. He was, Pete decided, more like Scratch than either of them realized. Winning was everything for both of them. The only difference was the tools they used.

Although the job title was a joke, Pete found that being known as the chief technical officer did have its uses. For starters, it gave him an excuse to make a big fuss over his "research" into the array's location. He threw himself into the role, wasting as much time as he could. He saved important geography and history books from the nation's biggest libraries – before they could be given away as firewood – and spent hours poring over them and making copious notes.

While doing so, he managed to convince the Arcturians that he was trying to piece together the next location after each new discovery, even though he already knew where all the sites were thanks to his conversation with Private Ross all those years ago in the space station above Hosin.

Whether the Arcturians believed him or not wasn't clear. Scratch seemed happy to go along with it, though, as long as he delivered a new piece with clockwork regularity. There had only been one misstep when he'd confused the Aztec pyramids in Mexico with the Mayan ones in Belize, resulting in an unnecessary dig and some angry complaints from the citizens of Mexico City. He still hadn't lived that one down.

Pete had hoped someone would use the time he'd bought by stalling over the array to fight back against the invasion. But no one did. He had been shocked to see the whole world surrender to the Arcturians within the first year of their arrival. Now here he was, slowly revealing the pieces of the ancient Squid artefact in the hope something would change before he was finished. Sometimes he wondered why he didn't just give it all up. Just dump all the pieces in their lap and walk away.

He knew the answer to that. It was *fear*. He was terrified of what he'd seen the Red Eyes do to those who opposed them. Whenever he thought of the mind-control devices and implants they'd used to torture Eldreth and Private Ross on the space station, he shuddered. It wasn't an experience he wanted. Better to listen to Xander and try and remain useful for as long as possible. Convince the enemy you were their friend.

After his last conversation with Scratch, though, he had a sinking feeling that the alien was onto him. Casey's return had definitely put the cat among the pigeons. In the past Scratch had been happy to let Pete play for time since it helped her consolidate her position in the Arcturian ranks. Now she was determined to have answers … and soon. Pete knew she was preparing to get rid of Xander. Perhaps she already had a plan to eventually get rid of him, too.

He sighed and headed up the mansion's curved staircase. Thinking about Casey's return was something that he found unsettling. For the longest time he'd hoped she was still on Hosin with the Squids and he had quietly prayed that she wasn't dead. Now that he knew she was back on Earth, he felt conflicted. He was relieved she was alive and, in some ways, he couldn't wait to see her again. Yet, he didn't want her to judge what he'd been doing these last few years. He knew she would accuse him of abandoning their mum and selling out by helping the Arcturians.

He closed his bedroom door. A dinner jacket, one that Xander had arranged for him, was lying on his bed ready for tonight's reception. The tailor, an elderly man with a Hungarian accent, had visited Pete a few weeks ago to fit him for it. The jacket and trousers he'd made were cut from the finest silk velvet. It was rich and luxurious and, as Pete put the suit on, he felt like he was papering himself in fifty-pound notes. It was probably the most expensive piece of clothing he'd ever worn.

He put it on and looked in the mirror. He barely recognized himself. He tucked the dog tags, the ones his dad had worn, into the neck of the crisp white shirt and then struggled with his black bow tie. It wasn't easy.

There was a rap at his door.

"Sir," the butler said from the other side, "the overseer is waiting for you downstairs."

Pete found Scratch in the hallway, pacing the checkerboard floor with her talons buried inside the long, drooping sleeves of her cowl. She looked up as Pete descended the staircase, her coal black eyes taking in his dinner jacket.

"Are we late?" he asked, checking the grandfather clock that stood in the corner. It was an ancient timepiece, wound daily by the equally ancient butler with a brass key. Pete was never sure how much he should trust it.

"We have time," the alien said. Then she added, "I looked over the information you sent me yesterday."

"And are you satisfied?" Pete asked, trying to keep his voice neutral.

"A most remarkable conclusion to our journey," Scratch said. She stepped closer to him. "You're quite certain about the location?"

"Yes, Overseer."

"Much rides on this, Peter. I need you to be sure."

"I am completely sure. That's where you'll find the final piece. Once you have it, you can control the array."

"Well, isn't this cosy?" Xander interrupted, appearing behind them. Lisa, the girl from the swimming pool, was draped on his arm. She wore a glittery black dress and had curled her hair. She broke off from Xander and checked her make-up in the hallway mirror. "You must be happy, Overseer?" Xander asked.

"Indeed," Scratch hissed. "Your chief technical officer has delivered everything we need to finish this."

"And what a surprise it is," Xander said and smiled that winning smile of his. His teeth were so white they lit up the room. "No one would have expected the final location would be at Stonehenge."

Scratch hissed and looked at Lisa warningly. She was applying a fresh coat of lip gloss in the mirror.

"Don't worry about her," Xander said airily. "She never listens to anything. Do you, Lisa?"

"What's that, hun?" the girl asked, meeting his gaze in the mirror.

Xander turned back to Scratch. "So, we can announce it?" he asked. "Tonight? At the party?"

"Tonight is the perfect time." Scratch nodded. "We are expecting a special guest. They will be thrilled to hear the news."

"What kind of special guest?" Xander asked, his brow furrowing. Pete knew he didn't like surprises. They made him feel powerless.

"The most special guest you can imagine," Scratch said and gave the Arcturian approximation of a smile. Pete shuddered. He'd learned from bitter experience that whenever Scratch looked happy, someone somewhere ended up suffering horribly. He just hoped it wouldn't be him.

The grandfather clock bonged the hour.

"Come on, babe," Xander told Lisa. "The car is waiting." The girl smacked her lips together in the mirror one final time and then took his arm.

As the others headed out to the limousine waiting on the driveway, Scratch lingered a moment with Pete. She touched the arm of his dinner jacket with her claw, stroking the silky material.

"It suits you, Peter," she murmured. "It makes you look grown up."

With a jolt, Pete realized that she was giving him a compliment.

"Thank you, Overseer."

"I haven't forgotten our agreement," the alien assured him. "You won't have to be chief technical officer for much longer. It's time for you to step out of Xander's shadow."

Pete gulped and followed her to the front door. The ancient butler stood beside it. He bowed low.

"Enjoy your evening, sir."

13

I DON'T KNOW HOW TO SPELL HORS D'OEUVRES, BUT THEY SURE DO TASTE GOOD

The country house reminded Casey of one of those boring National Trust places her parents had dragged her around when she was little. Its exterior was covered in thick, red ivy. The inside was full of enormous, high-ceilinged rooms and huge windows that looked out over manicured lawns and gravel paths. Each room was decorated with stag heads, Arabian rugs and antique furniture. The house had once belonged to some distant cousin of the Queen. Now, like everything else on the planet, it belonged to the Red Eyes.

Marcel and his team of chefs had spent all day in the basement kitchens preparing dishes for the reception. A five-course meal was on the menu for the evening, along with champagne and canapés beforehand. The head cook's face grew increasingly red as he ordered his staff about, one eye constantly on the clock. There were a hundred guests on the invite list – not counting their plus ones – and the caterers were working with feverish haste to get everything ready.

While the food was being prepared, Casey and her friends had time to plan their mission. Cheeze requisitioned a quiet corner of the storeroom and tapped away on the computer built into his hoverchair, hacking into the building's surveillance systems. A grid of camera feeds appeared on his monitor giving him a view of every room in the house and several angles on the grounds as well.

"I'll be your eyes and ears while the party's on," he told Casey and the others as they stood in their waiting staff outfits – black trousers, crisp white shirts and gold-embroidered waistcoats. "Although I'm gutted I won't get to join you out there. Those penguin suits are sick."

"Laugh it up, tech-head," Fish growled, tugging at the hem of his too-small waistcoat in irritation.

"Here, Alastair," Marguerite said, adjusting the strap on the back and letting it out a little. "Let me give you some room to breathe."

Fish reddened. "Thanks," he mumbled. He gave Cheeze a hard stare, challenging him to say anything. The hacker suppressed a laugh and turned back to his screens.

Casey, preoccupied with the mission, ran through the plan one more time.

"When Commander Deacon arrives in the ballroom, we need to move quickly," she told the group. "We steal his passkey, then Baba will clone it. Soon as that's done, we'll slip it back in his pocket before he notices it's gone. Then we'll pack up and head out via the service corridor that leads to the kitchen."

"How are we supposed to get his passkey, though?" Brain asked warily. "Pickpocketing is an art. You don't just shove your hands into someone's trousers and pull out their wallet without them noticing."

"Maybe we should just kidnap him," Jude suggested, her eyes glinting at the thrill of it. "Take the key *and* its owner."

"And have every Red Cap in London after us?" Casey shook her head. "We need to stay hidden. If we're busted, it's Game Over."

The weight of that hit them and their banter dried up. They all knew they were steaming ahead with a plan that they'd thrown together on the hoof. So much could go wrong ... and if it did, the consequences could be lethal.

"Here," Haruto said, interrupting the silence. "We're gonna need comms." He handed out discreet earpieces and throat mics.

"Where did you get these?" Casey asked.

"I borrowed them off some Red Cap soldiers last week. Best not to know the details."

As the team tested their mics, Fish picked up a menu for the banquet and studied it with a hungry eye. It was written in a fancy, swirly font. "What are 'horse doors'?" he asked.

"*Hors d'oeuvres*," Marguerite corrected him in a flawless French accent. "They're those little appetizers that you get at fancy parties. My parents work in catering," she explained.

"Really?" Fish asked. "My dad runs a chip shop. I guess we're, like, in the same industry."

Cheeze stifled a laugh. Fish shot him a death glare.

The party was a lavish event. The guests arrived in a fleet of chauffeur-driven limousines. The Red Cap commanders wore black military dress uniforms with silver stars on their starched collars. Various corporate leaders and CEOs also attended, all in black tie and expensive ballgowns. Several Arcturian overseers joined the crowd wearing their traditional monk-like cowls. The invaders seemed to have become part of the landscape, their presence accepted by the humans without a second thought.

As the guests mingled in the ballroom under a huge chandelier, Casey and her friends wove through the crowd carrying silver trays loaded with champagne flutes and canapés. A string quartet played in the corner and the classical music that emanated from them gave the proceedings a refined and civilized air. Floor to ceiling windows at the far end of the ballroom looked out over the house's impressive grounds, while the centrepiece of the room was a huge ice sculpture carved in the shape of an Arcturian helmet.

"It's like a James Bond movie," Elite said over the comms as the Reapers fanned out through the crowd pretending to be servers.

"007 – but with aliens," Brain replied.

"I've never seen so many overseers all in one place," Haruto commented. "Imagine if the Resistance launched an attack here. We could take out most of the senior leadership. Maybe even end the occupation for good."

"Tempting," Jude murmured into her mic.

"We don't have the weapons or the manpower for something like that," Casey reminded them. "Let's focus on finding Commander Deacon."

Haruto grunted over the comms, which she took to mean he agreed, albeit reluctantly.

As she worked her way through the ballroom, Casey stopped here and there to offer guests a champagne flute from her tray. Most took one without even giving her a second glance. Being a server made her invisible, which, given her mission, was exactly what she needed. As she passed a couple of businessmen, she caught a bit of their conversation.

"Say what you want about the Arcturians," one remarked to the other, "but my net worth is up twenty-seven per cent this year alone. They're making all the right people rich."

"I'll drink to that!" his friend laughed and grabbed two glasses from Casey's tray. Casey nodded and smiled, fighting back her repulsion. How could these people sell out their fellow citizens to the aliens?

Cheeze's voice on the comms interrupted her train of thought.

"Has anyone got a visual on the commander yet?" he asked from his position in the kitchens, watching the camera feeds on his monitors. "He's not on any of my screens."

"The dude's not very tall," Elite said, remembering what Casey had told them about her encounter with the diminutive commander at her mum's house. "Maybe he's hidden by the crowd."

"Me and Marguerite will watch the main door," Babatunde said. "You keep circulating."

Casey was about to reply when a hand fell on her shoulder.

"Miss? Can I trouble you for a glass of champagne?"

Casey turned to see her mum. She was wearing a sleek black cocktail dress, simple but elegant. Casey stared at her in awe. She'd never seen her mum dressed up like this. She looked beautiful. "I had to let it out a bit," Mum whispered, smoothing down the dress, oblivious to her daughter's amazement.

"Where's the commander?" Casey asked.

"He stopped to speak to someone. He'll be here in a minute. What do you need me to do exactly?"

"You have to get his passkey, the one that he uses to order inventory from the supply depot. We only need it for a few minutes so we can clone it. Do you think you can manage that?"

"Easy," Mum replied. "He loves showing off about that warehouse of his. Just leave it to me."

A voice behind interrupted.

"There you are, Rebecca!" Commander Deacon exclaimed, his face beetroot purple with exertion. "I thought I'd lost you." He mopped his brow with a handkerchief, flustered.

"Oh, you won't lose me, Herbert," Mum laughed. "I intend to stick to you like glue tonight." She linked her arm through his. The height difference between them made them look like a comedy double act.

"You've found the bubbly!" the commander exclaimed, noticing Casey's tray. "As if you weren't bubbly enough already, my dear!" He took the last two glasses.

"Oh, Herbert, you are funny!" Mum giggled obligingly.

Casey looked at the commander a moment, wondering where his passkey could be. In his pocket? His wallet? This plan suddenly seemed much harder than when they'd discussed it downstairs in the kitchen. He noticed her staring and reddened.

"Stop gawping and fill up your tray, girl," he told her snippily. Casey nodded and slunk away. "You just can't get good staff these days," she heard him complain as she departed.

Casey headed back into the crowd and tapped her comms on. "Mum's with him," she told the boys.

"Give them a minute," Brain said. "I'll circle around and see what happens. It'll look less suspicious if it's a new server." He paused to attend to a group of overseers grunting away in Arcturian. They took cups of *klaart* from his tray with their taloned claws.

Casey moved to the back of the room to restock her tray. She tried her best to not stare as her mum flirted with the commander. Seeing her here, helping them fight the invaders, Casey felt an overwhelming burst of pride.

At the back of the ballroom, Casey found Fish manning the buffet table. A few hungry guests were filling plates. When no one was looking Fish snaffled a few canapés.

"Any luck?" he asked, brushing crumbs from his server's uniform to hide the evidence.

"Mum's working her magic," Casey said. "You know you're supposed to be serving the food not eating it, right?"

"I have a high metabolism. Besides, these horse door things are delish. Try the round ones, they're really good." He shoved another couple in his mouth. "Baba and Marguerite have gone to the kitchen for more."

A hand brushed Casey's arm.

"This food looks delicious," Mum said to no one in particular. She took a plate and selected a few of the tasty treats. When she was sure no one was listening, she dropped her voice low. "We've got a problem, Casey. The commander doesn't keep the passkey in his pocket."

"You'll have to steal his wallet, then."

"No, Casey, you don't understand. He wears the passkey around his neck on a lanyard. He says that way he can never leave home without it. I don't know how I can get it off him. Not without him realizing…"

"That's not good," Casey said, concerned. "Let me talk to the others. In the meantime, keep him sweet until we come up with something."

Mum smiled, impressed by her daughter's tenacity. "Your dad used to say that if Plan A doesn't work out you still have twenty-five letters of the alphabet left."

Casey nodded, grateful for her mum's support, but uncertain how going through her ABCs would help.

"Let's hope nothing else goes wrong," she said.

There was a commotion behind them as the ballroom doors opened and six imperial guards in white power armour entered the room. Behind them strode a tall, regal figure.

"Oh, no," Casey cried, turning pale. "It's the emperor!"

14

GUEST OF HONOUR

The Arcturians' supreme leader strode into the ballroom, his red cloak flowing behind. His imperial guard fanned out around him, creating a protective ring. The audience looked on in stunned, fearful silence. The musicians in the string quartet stopped playing mid-recital, uncertain of the correct etiquette.

The emperor basked in the attention for a moment. Then, with a flourish, he removed his distinctive helmet to reveal his pinched and scaly face. A frill of leather skin puffed out around his neck like an Elizabethan ruff, giving him an imperious air. The overseers in the audience bowed their heads low and the humans, scared of causing offence, did the same. Few people on Earth had ever set eyes on the Arcturian leader and no one was quite sure of the correct protocol.

"What's he doing here?" Haruto said over the

comms. "He wasn't supposed to leave the space station until the final piece of the array was excavated."

"Their schedule must be moving faster than we thought," Brain replied, coming onto the voice channel.

"Or our intel was bad," Cheeze added, still watching everything on his monitor from the kitchens.

"Maybe it's a sign," Haruto said, his voice hardening. "Maybe we should take him out right here, right now."

"What are we gonna attack him with?" Casey hissed. "Canapés?" She didn't need him flying off the handle.

"We're here for the passkey," Brain reminded him. "Nothing else."

"Stuff the passkey," Haruto growled.

Looking across the room, Casey saw the boy draw his plasma pistol. He slid it under the white serving cloth that lay draped across his arm.

"You'll be dead before you can fire a shot," she warned him over the comms. "If we get the passkey we can take the *Blocka* servers offline and stop the Arcturians from accessing the array. Stick to the plan!"

"Do you know how long I've waited for this moment?" Haruto said. "I might never get another chance like this."

"Haruto's right," Babatunde's deep voice chipped in. "This is a gift."

"It's suicide!" Jude warned.

The boy didn't reply. Instead, he moved across the ballroom, easing his way through the crowd. No one paid him any attention. All eyes were on the emperor.

"Look how many troops are with him," Casey said over the comms. "I know how much you hate the emperor, but you'll be dead before you even pull the trigger. Don't let your anger blind you."

"Then use those powers of yours," Haruto snapped, glaring across the crowded ballroom at her. "All I keep hearing about is how amazing the great gamer **CASEY_FLOW** is. How she can lift cars in the air and throw them with her bare hands like some kind of superhero. Well, now's the time! Their leader is right here. You can kill him."

"It doesn't work like that," Casey said, speaking so loudly into her mic that she drew stares from a group of commanders and their wives standing near by. She turned away and dropped her voice. "It's not like I can just push a button. It's ... not completely in my control."

Casey swallowed, aware that it sounded like a cop-out. The truth was, though, Haruto's anger troubled her. She'd sensed its power when she'd reached into his mind, and she could see how his desire for revenge clouded his judgement. She'd felt anger like that herself: once after her dad had died; and again when the Red

Eyes had killed Eldreth, Dreyfus and Private Ross on the space station above Hosin. What disturbed her the most, though, was that it reminded her of how she felt about her brother's betrayal.

She looked across the ballroom at Haruto, silently pleading with him to reconsider. His voice fumed in her ear in response.

"You might be too scared to act, Casey, but I'm not."

There was a beep on the channel as Haruto dropped out of the voice chat. He pulled his comms device from his ear and strode through the crowd of commanders and overseers. The barrel of his plasma pistol pointed out from under the white server's cloth on his arm. Casey knew there was no way he would be able to get past the imperial guards. An assassination attempt like this was madness.

At that moment the lights in the ballroom dimmed. Everyone froze in anticipation, including Haruto. Casey seized the opportunity to head in his direction, hoping to intercept him before he could pull the trigger. She'd only taken a few steps when there was a burst of sound and light on the stage at the far end of the ballroom.

A thudding bass announced the arrival of ... Xander! The YouTuber bounced onto the stage. His teeth, polished to a blinding whiteness by some celebrity dentist, flashed under the ballroom's crystal chandelier as he smiled at the crowd. Behind him, hiding from the limelight, was Pete.

Casey froze. This was the first time she'd seen her little brother in the flesh since she'd returned home. She stared at him, overcome with conflicting emotions. He looked so different. It wasn't just the dinner jacket; it was his whole demeanour. He was no longer her kid brother, he was a gangly teenage boy. He seemed as alien to her as the invaders.

She caught sight of her mum in the crowd. She had her hand over her mouth as if in shock. Tears streaked down her cheeks, making her mascara run. Casey prayed she wouldn't try and call out to Pete, or rush to the stage. That could only end in disaster.

"Ladies, gentlemen and esteemed Arcturian guests," Xander began, casting his eye across the ballroom to the emperor and bowing low. "It is an honour to address you all tonight. A night that will go down in the history books of our two planets." There was a ripple of excited applause from the humans in the audience. "I am here to announce that we are on the verge of completing our mission. Thanks to the hard work of our chief technical officer –" here Xander gestured to Pete – "the final piece of the array is almost in our grasp."

More applause and some excited hollering from the

human commanders. The Arcturians looked on, their obsidian eyes cold and calculating. Casey wondered how Pete was feeling. He stood stock still with his head bowed. He certainly didn't look proud of the achievement. Perhaps he regretted selling the universe down the river.

"We have travelled to the four corners of the Earth searching for this ancient artefact," Xander continued. "But now that journey is over..."

He paused theatrically as the crowd murmured in anticipation. Casey could see why the Red Eyes had thought he was valuable. He was a natural showman.

There was a flicker and a huge screen behind Xander lit up. The guests gasped in astonishment, recognizing the image it displayed.

"The standing stones of Stonehenge have been the stuff of myth and legend for thousands of years," Xander continued. "Tonight, we will reveal the truth behind them ... or perhaps I should say *beneath* them."

The camera burrowed underground to reveal a huge spaceship lying dormant under the stone circle. It was an enormous piece of alien tech, with a curved, circular body that gave way to a finned front section in the shape of a double-headed axe. The ship was about the size of two football pitches and it made the giant stones above the ground look like pebbles. It lay underground as if waiting to be awakened – an extraterrestrial Sleeping Beauty.

Xander let the audience take it all in before he continued. "This ancient Bactu vessel, hidden for millennia beneath our feet, is the control centre for the array. Once it is in our possession, nothing will stop our Arcturian allies from bringing order to the universe. Glory to Arcturia!"

With that Xander turned to the emperor and bowed once again.

"A toast!" a man shouted from the audience. Casey recognized him from the TV. He had once been a rising star in the government, tipped to be Prime Minister. She guessed his hopes had been dashed by the arrival of the Arcturians. Still, he seemed happy enough to curry favour with the invaders. "To our Arcturian allies. May their quest end fruitfully!" he cried and lifted his champagne glass.

"To our Arcturian allies!" the humans cheered. The overseers and the emperor looked on, bemused by this human tradition of raising drinks into the air. None of them lifted their cups of *klaart*.

Seizing the moment, Casey hurried after Haruto, pushing through the crowd as quickly as she dared. There was a screech as her earpiece released a burst of static. She winced. Through the feedback she could hear Cheeze's panicked voice saying something, his words garbled.

"Cheeze," she said into her mic. "Repeat that. You're breaking up."

"… coming … run!" cried her friend.

Casey tensed. Something was very wrong.

Across the ballroom she could see the rest of the Reapers in their waiters' uniforms. They were spread out, covering the doors. They looked at one another, panicked. Haruto was in the middle of the ballroom now, negotiating a path through the crowd towards the emperor. He'd ditched his earpiece and had no idea anything was wrong.

Casey charged forward, pushing a commander out of her way and ignoring his cries of complaint. She had to stop Haruto.

Before she could get to him, ten Arcturian grunts burst into the room, armed and ready for combat. The imperial guard reacted instantly, encircling the emperor and drawing their lances from their belts in case this was some kind of attempted coup against their leader. The high-tech spears expanded in their hands and the troops spun them in sweeping circles through the air like martial artists. The Red Eye grunts ignored them, fanning out along the edge of the ballroom with their weapons ready.

Scratch followed them into the room and threw her

hood back to reveal her reptilian features. She bowed low to the emperor.

"Forgive the intrusion, Exalted One. We have a security situation. Members of the Resistance have infiltrated the building." Behind Scratch, Babatunde and Marguerite were led in, their hands shackled. "These terrorists are on our Most Wanted list," Scratch continued. "They were seen attacking a checkpoint a few days ago. We suspect they're not alone here."

"Marguerite," Fish whispered, distraught at seeing the redheaded girl captured.

"Arrest all the waiters!" Scratch ordered her troops.

Realizing the game was up, Haruto burst forward and raised his plasma pistol. His first shot was illjudged, hitting an imperial guard in the shoulder and knocking him off his feet. He was about to take a second shot when a Red Eye came up behind him and smacked him between his shoulder blades with the butt of his plasma rifle.

"Haruto!" Jude cried as he hit the floor.

Cheeze's voice was back on the comms, clearer this time. "One of the commanders recognized Baba and Marguerite from the checkpoint," he warned. "They've got Marcel and the other kitchen staff in custody. We're busted. Everyone, get out! NOW!"

Casey knew they had to move. The problem was

that the Red Eyes had every exit covered. She looked at the vast windows overlooking the gardens. It was the only way out that wasn't guarded by guns.

"Head for the windows!" she yelled into her mic.

"But they're shut!" Brain replied in her ear.

"Just trust me."

"What about Marguerite?" Fish fretted. "We can't leave her ... or Baba."

"We haven't got a choice!"

Scratch stepped forward and scanned the crowd. "Where's the girl? Where is *Cay-See*?" The ballroom lights glinted off the alien's scales as she looked around. The guests turned to one another, uncertain who she was talking about.

"I'm here!" Casey shouted, hoping to buy her friends an extra second or two to get to the windows. The crowd parted around her. She caught sight of Pete onstage staring at her with flinty eyes. He had chosen his side, she realized.

Scratch motioned to her troops and three Red Eyes approached Casey as the horrified guests looked on. Two aliens put their guns on her. The third held a strange device in his hands, a thin band of black metal. It reminded her of the device the Arcturians had fitted to Eldreth to block his psi-powers.

A feeling of dread tingled along her spine, made

all the worse by the smirk of anticipation she saw on Scratch's lizard lips. Casey guessed what the device would do to her. She took a step back. Two human commanders blocked her path. They grabbed her arms and pinned them behind her back.

No, Casey thought. *I will not let this happen.*

The ballroom seemed to get smaller. Casey felt her body tense. Time slowed and her mind focussed. She felt the familiar sensation of flow crackling through her body again, filling every cell. The two men holding her arms behind her back must have felt it too because they suddenly let go of her as if they'd been stung.

The approaching Red Eyes didn't give up so easily. The one carrying the headband reached for her, perhaps hoping to get the device in place before she could stop him. The mechanical red eyes set in his black helmet burned intensely.

She raised her hands in the air and a circular blast of invisible energy burst out, knocking the Red Eyes and several commanders off their feet like dominoes. In the confusion, a plasma rifle discharged into the air and blasted a huge chunk out of the ornate ceiling above them. It knocked the glass chandelier from its mountings and the glass monstrosity fell to the ballroom floor in a sweeping crash. The crowd screamed and scattered in panic.

"Now!" Casey shouted to her friends. "Run for the windows!"

The Reapers hurtled through the chaos, sprinting towards the enormous bay window that looked out onto the gardens. Haruto managed to get back on his feet and limped after them, injured but determined. Jude grabbed his hand and dragged him along. Somewhere, deep in the basement of the building, Casey heard the muffled sound of Cheeze's hoverchair firing. It was all kicking off!

As her friends ran for the windows, Casey stretched out her hands in a wide arc. The air crackled around her, and that same invisible power swept through the ballroom in an almighty rush of air. The bay window smashed open, blowing the glass out across the lawn. She saw Brain and then Fish dive through what was left of the frame.

Casey made to run after them, but her legs buckled underneath her. Using her powers twice in quick succession had left her weak. She willed herself on, desperate to get away. She might have made it, too, if a hand hadn't grabbed her wrist.

"I've got her, Your Excellency!" Commander Deacon shouted triumphantly, looking over at the emperor. "I have the girl!" He put Casey in a half-nelson. It felt as if he was about to break her arm. She screamed in pain.

"Get your hands off my daughter!" Casey's mum cried. She threw herself at the commander, taking him totally by surprise. Casey was shocked too. She'd never seen her mum this angry.

"Rebecca? What are you doing?!" the commander cried. He was clearly regretting his choice of plus one for tonight's event.

"This date is over," Mum said. Pulling up her cocktail dress she slammed her knee hard into the commander's groin. He whimpered in shock and pain and fell to the floor. In a swift movement Mum yanked the lanyard off his neck and tossed it across the ballroom. Elite caught it in mid-air as he sprinted for the window.

Casey watched as the rest of her friends jumped through the broken glass and crashed onto the lawn. Before she could follow them, a squad of Red Eyes surrounded her. Casey felt the aliens' gloved hands grab her and slam her face first into the ballroom floor.

"I love you, Casey!" Mum shouted as she was bundled away by the Arcturians. "Don't ever forget that."

"No!" Casey yelled, struggling against the Red Eyes. She needed to find some last scrap of flow power to use against them. Nothing came. She looked up at the stage, hoping Pete would come to her rescue. But her brother – along with Xander and the emperor – had already been ushered out of the ballroom to safety.

Something cold and hard pressed against Casey's forehead, squeezing tight against her skin. Scratch's face appeared right beside her ear, her sharp talons fitting the Arcturian device to Casey's head and tightening it mercilessly. The ballroom seemed to recede, glitching and fading away like a bad videocall connection.

"Sweet dreams," the alien whispered, and then everything went dark.

15

NOW THAT WAS A PARTY

Pete stood in silence on the gravel in front of the country house. He watched as the prisoners were frogmarched away one by one. His sister was loaded into a black prisoner transport van. She hung her head, either too angry or too exhausted to meet his gaze. Nothing about her seemed to have changed since he'd last seen her. She had the same blue hair, even the same clothes. It was like she'd been frozen in time the last four years.

"How does it feel to see your sister finally being brought to heel?" Scratch asked, appearing beside him. She had the hood of her cowl up and Pete couldn't see her face, but he suspected she was testing him somehow. Pete knew the Arcturians valued loyalty more than anything. He wasn't quite sure how to answer her. He had, after all, betrayed his own flesh and blood.

"I don't think she's my sister any more," Pete replied

eventually. "She's not the same person."

"Explain."

"Something happened to her when she met the Bactu," Pete continued. He hoped that the mention of the Arcturians' ancient enemies would distract Scratch. "They did something to her. She's changed."

"Interesting," the alien hissed. "Does this mean your *Cay-See* no longer deserves your loyalty?"

Pete bit his lip a moment. "On Arcturia, when a sibling betrays another it cuts all bonds of family for ever, isn't that right?" He hoped he'd remembered correctly.

"Very true, Peter, very true."

"Well, the bond between me and Casey is cut now too," he told her flatly. "She has sided with the Bactu." Scratch grunted. Pete took it as a good sign. "The one person who could have stopped you is now your prisoner," he continued. "You've won, Overseer."

Scratch removed her hood. "Arcturia has won," she corrected. "I am merely its humble servant." Despite her words, her snake face beamed with delight.

"What happens next?"

"We will interrogate your sister. Find out everything she knows about the Resistance's plans. With any luck she will identify the informant."

"Do you have any idea who it is?"

Scratch grunted. "I have my suspicions." The alien moved closer to him, making his skin crawl. He fought the urge to bolt. "Don't you?"

Pete shifted his weight from one foot to the other. "I guess it has to be someone with access and influence," he mused. "But also, ambition. Maybe they thought the Resistance had a chance of overthrowing the occupation and they were hoping to be in charge when it happened. They'd be wrong, of course," he added hurriedly. "Arcturia is ascendant. Always."

Scratch's black eyes were impossible to read. "Do you suspect someone in particular, Peter?"

Pete thought for a moment. "It would have to be someone who likes to play both sides," he said. "And they'd need a big ego to believe they could get away with it." His eyes drifted to Xander. A couple of starstruck Red Caps were taking a selfie with him. The YouTuber posed, crossing his index fingers into his "X" trademark. Whatever admiration Pete had once felt for him had long since withered and died. The last four years had been a slow descent into contempt for his former idol. Never meet your heroes, they said. It was true.

Scratch pulled her hood over her head and then slipped her talons into the sleeves of her cowl. "That boy's ego is his greatest asset and his biggest flaw. If your hunch proves to be right, I will deal with him."

"Overseer," Pete said as the alien turned to leave. "Let me talk to Casey. Maybe I can get through to her. Family matters to us humans."

Scratch laughed mirthlessly. "It matters to Arcturians, too."

"Really?"

"Why do you think I am here, so far from home, Peter? I have three children back on Arcturia. Three children who can only advance if their mother advances. Each promotion I earn brings them up with me. My glory is their glory."

"I never realized you had kids," Pete said, unable to hide his surprise. He'd never seen an Arcturian child and assumed they were all back on the home planet being trained for combat until they came of age and joined the ranks of the Red Eyes. He couldn't imagine Scratch as a mother. Not even an absent one.

"Talk to your sister," Scratch ordered. "Maybe she will do the right thing for her little brother before you cut the ties between you for ever. If she doesn't, the next person she will see is me."

The alien headed off, crunching across the gravel. Pete knew she would be rewarded for stopping the Resistance, and perhaps those children of hers would move up a rung or two on the Arcturian social ladder. But if she really wanted to win the emperor's favour, revealing an informer within the ranks of the occupation would be quite a result. She would be lavished with promotions and glory. He shuddered at the thought of her gaining any more power.

"Hey, kid," Xander said, coming over to him. "Helluva party, amirite?"

Pete fixed a smile on his face. "You bet. Ice sculptures, canapés, terrorists ... it had it all."

Xander bristled, sensing the sarcasm in his voice.

"A pity your sister had to come along and mess it all up. If we're not careful, she'll ruin everything. We haven't worked this hard for Casey to spoil things. The Arcturians have been good to us."

"They've been good to *you*," Pete retorted. "They gave you everything you wanted. A mansion, money and a global platform."

"You got what you wanted too," Xander reminded him. "You asked for your mum to be protected. Well, the Red Eyes didn't put her on the dig crews. They kept her out of all that and let her carry on working at the hospital. But here is your dear old mum, arrested in the middle of a Resistance plot to kill the emperor. Who knows what will happen to her now? And it's all thanks to that crazy sister of yours. I've told you this a million times ... Casey is a liability."

Pete poked the gravel on the driveway with his

shoe. "Do you ever ask yourself if the Resistance might be right?" he asked. "Like maybe they're fighting for the right thing?"

"If I did, would I admit it?" Xander replied, chuckling to himself. "I keep telling you, kid, you gotta keep your cards close to your chest. It's the only way to survive in this crazy world."

Pete looked across the driveway as the doors on the prisoner transport van slammed shut with a heavy clang. It drove off, its wheels crunching over the gravel. He decided to bury his emotions, just like Xander had taught him.

One day his friend would realize just how good he'd become at it.

16

I, FOR ONE, WELCOME OUR NEW ALIEN OVERLORDS

Casey's cell in the police station was bare and functional. There was a stainless steel toilet and sink in the corner. A simple bed, comprised of a concrete shelf and a thin piece of foam mattress, was fitted against the wall. It was nothing like the futuristic prison cell on the space station. The Red Eyes clearly weren't interested in sharing their technology with their human allies.

Casey sat on the edge of the bed, touching the metal band on her head. It was tight and painful, and it squeezed her temples like a vice. She let her fingertips play over it, uncertain how it worked. She could tell it was blocking the abilities the Squids had unlocked inside her brain, robbing her of her "flow". It was like when you lost all your power-ups in *Super Mario Bros.*, she thought. She was back to being Casey again.

Boring, plain old vanilla Casey.

She wasn't sure how long she'd been in the cell. Time seemed to lose its meaning when you were stuck in a room with nothing to do, no book to read or mobile phone to tap. She waited, lost in her own thoughts. Eventually, there was a jangle of keys in the corridor outside her cell. The viewing slit in the heavy door opened and a woman peered through.

"You have a visitor," the guard said. "Stand with your back against the wall." She slammed the hatch shut. "Five minutes," she told someone outside the door. There was a click as the lock was turned and the door swung open. The guard stood to the side, one hand on her stun baton, as Pete brushed past her. "If you need anything, just shout." She closed and locked the door behind him.

Casey stared at her brother, speechless. This was the first time she'd seen him up close since she'd returned to Earth. She was struck by how much he had changed during the years she'd spent lost in hyperspace. His face had narrowed, his cheekbones more pronounced than ever before. He looked gaunt and pale, and his skin had erupted with teenage spots. He was several centimetres taller than her, too, which was weird because he'd always been small for his age.

"Hello to you too, big sis," Pete said, breaking the uncomfortable silence. She noted his voice had broken. He really wasn't her kid brother any more, she decided.

Maybe, after all that had happened, he wasn't even her brother. Her face flushed with anger. For her the events on Hosin were just a few days old. They were raw and recent. For him, they were ancient history; things that had happened years ago.

Another silence hung between them. Pete stared at the band around her forehead and then, as if embarrassed, his eyes flitted away. His gaze fell on the toilet. It didn't have a seat and it looked like it hadn't been cleaned since the last occupant. Or maybe even the one before. He grimaced in disgust.

"They told me the Ritz was fully booked," Casey said.

"Maybe I can talk to them about transferring you somewhere better," Pete offered.

Casey's face flashed with fury. "You can do that, can you?"

"Of course!"

"And how come you – my kid brother – can talk to the Red Eyes about how they treat their prisoners?"

Pete shook his head. "You don't understand, Casey."

"Oh, I understand *everything*," she told him. "You and Xander made a deal with the Red Eyes. You sold out."

"That's not true!"

"You betrayed everyone. Me, Mum … the planet."

"You're wrong!"

The surveillance camera on the ceiling whirred and twisted on its mount, reminding them both that they were being watched. Pete took a breath and lowered his voice. "I did what I thought was best, for everyone."

"And now you've come to gloat?"

"I'm here because they want answers from you. They want to know about your powers. Most of all, though, they want to know about the Resistance."

"I'm not going to sell out my friends. I'm not like you."

Pete recoiled from her words. "I know I've made mistakes," he whispered. "But the Arcturians are in charge here, not me. If you tell them everything you know about the Resistance's network, they'll go easy on you ... and Mum, too."

The mention of their mum got Casey's attention. "Have you seen her? Is she OK?"

Pete's face clouded. "She's under house arrest."

"What about my friends? Marguerite? Babatunde?"

"They're prisoners too."

"Are they here?"

"They've been sent to join the dig crews." Pete ran a hand over the back of his neck, rubbing at his tense muscles. "I'm sorry, Casey. This isn't how I wanted things to turn out."

Casey stared at her brother. She thought about what

the last few years must have been like for him. It must have been awful watching Earth fall to the invaders. No wonder he looked so gaunt and pale. He'd lost his family and his planet… Most of all, he'd lost himself.

"Why did you help the Red Eyes?" she demanded.

Pete glanced at the surveillance camera before answering. "Because I didn't know what else to do. You were gone. No one was doing anything. I thought… Well, I thought things would turn out differently." He sighed and shook his head. "Just tell me what you know about the Resistance, and then I can try and help you and Mum. Did they tell you who the mole is? Who's giving them information?"

Casey shrugged.

"It will be much easier if you help them," said Pete.

"Will it?" Casey's tone was icy.

Pete shook his head, disappointed. "Do you remember the sign you used to have on your bedroom door, Casey? The one that said: WARNING: NO STUPID PEOPLE BEYOND THIS POINT?"

"Yeah. You never used to pay any attention to it."

"Maybe that's because stupid people never realize they're being stupid. They always think they're the smart ones."

The ghost of a smile passed over Casey's lips. "Good excuse."

"Right now, you think you're being smart. But you're really not. You're just too stupid to see it."

Casey straightened up, annoyed. "I guess we're done here, then."

"I was afraid you'd say that," her brother replied. He walked over to the cell door and rapped on it. The surveillance camera turned on its mount to watch him. "It's out of my hands now. Goodbye, Casey."

The guard unlocked the door and Pete slipped out. The door swung shut behind him. Casey was alone in her cell again. She couldn't help feeling that she'd just made a terrible mistake.

17

WE HAVE WAYS OF MAKING YOU SQUAWK

Casey wasn't sure how many hours passed between Pete leaving and her next visitor arriving. She slept intermittently and was fed with a tray of green and brown nutritional paste pushed through a hatch in the door by a young male guard. He smiled at her as she took it and offered her a cup of tea. It was the first bit of kindness anyone had shown her since she'd arrived.

She could cope with the boredom. She had even got used to the tightness of the band around her head. It was the feeling of failure that haunted her. She couldn't shake the sense that she'd let everyone down. She tried to cheer herself up by remembering that her teammates had escaped. Perhaps they could find a way to stop the Arcturians without her. The only thing she had to do was make sure she didn't give them away.

The door to her cell opened without warning and

two guards – a different man and the stern woman she'd seen earlier – entered. They hauled her off the bed, cuffed her hands behind her back, and then frogmarched her through the police station. Casey submitted, realizing she was powerless.

"Put her in here," the female guard told her colleague, opening the door to a poorly lit interrogation room. A low-slung leather seat, like a dentist's chair, stood in the middle of the room. Above it hung a bright light. It was angled so that the four corners of the room were left shrouded in darkness. Casey could see the outline of some kind of bulky equipment stacked against the walls. Before she could work out what it was, the guards uncuffed her and pushed her into the chair. The moment she sat in it, metal clamps snapped around her ankles and wrists, locking her in place.

"What's going on?" Casey asked, scared. The guards ignored her and retreated out of the door. "Wait!" she yelled desperately. "You can't just leave me here."

"Hello, *Cay-See*," Scratch hissed. Casey twisted in her chair, trying to see the figure that loomed behind her. Before she could, the chair tipped backwards, and she found herself lying flat on her back staring at the ceiling. The light above her burned into her pupils, creating a halo in her vision.

"What do you want?" Casey demanded, straining

against the straps. They were too tight. She felt utterly helpless.

"You know what I want," Scratch replied, her lizard eyes blinking sideways. "I want answers. Tell me about the Resistance." The alien's forked tongue flickered between her lips. "And, after that, you can tell me about you…"

Casey blinked into the blinding light, confused. "Me? What do you want to know about me?"

Scratch darted forward and placed her face directly in front of Casey's. Up close her scales gave off a musty smell, like rotting cucumbers. A long time ago, Casey had held a python at a friend's animal-themed birthday party. The reptile had curled around her neck, overpowering her with its musky stench. The Animal Man doing the show told her it was the creature's natural defence mechanism.

"Something happened to you on Hosin, didn't it?" Scratch hissed, her snake eyes narrowing as she peered into the girl's face in search of answers.

"I don't know what you're talking about," Casey lied, stalling for time.

"We've never seen a human with powers like yours," the alien continued, an edge in her voice. "What did the Bactu do to you? Tell me!"

"You're jealous!" Casey cried, suddenly realizing.

"Be careful, child," the alien hissed sharply.

Casey knew she'd touched a nerve. "Xolotl said the human race has untapped power," she continued. "They want us to be their heirs, not you." She wasn't sure if this was strictly true, but she was willing to go all in on it to annoy her Arcturian adversary.

"Enough!" Scratch yelled.

"Even if you do power up the array," Casey continued, "you won't ever get the Squids' power. You won't ever be like them ... or like me."

"Foolish girl," the alien muttered. "We have been fighting the Bactu for almost a hundred of your Earth years. Do you think we've learned nothing? Our technology is already catching up with their psi abilities. You saw how we enslaved your gamer friends on Hosin, controlling their minds with our devices, didn't you?"

Casey refused to answer, uncertain where this conversation was going. The metal band around her forehead felt like it was tightening.

"Would you like to see what else we've replicated?" Scratch asked. The alien swept away, vanishing out of her field of vision. Casey strained her neck trying to see what was happening. She felt prone and vulnerable strapped into this chair. She'd always hated visiting the dentist. This was a million times worse.

Scratch reappeared with a clutch of cables in her talons. She fitted them into a data port on the metal band around Casey's forehead, enjoying the fear she saw in the girl's eyes.

"Perhaps you should make a deal," the alien suggested, deliberately taking her time as she organized the cables. The wires stretched off into the darkness, connecting to some device that Casey couldn't see. "Your brother did a deal with us and look at him now. He has gone up in the world."

"I'll never make a deal with you," Casey spat. "Not even if my life depended on it."

"Such a brave child." Scratch's talons stroked Casey's cheek. They were black as ebony and their curved points were rough and chipped, worn with use. "But everyone has a breaking point. Even you…"

Scratch spun Casey's chair around so she could see the far side of the room. An enormous computer system was set into the rear wall, its blue LED lights blinking on and off. Inside the casing Casey could see motherboards stacked one on top of another. It reminded her of the inside of a beehive. It looked incredibly powerful.

"If you won't tell me your secrets willingly," Scratch continued, "I'll have no choice but to get them myself."

The alien tapped a control console and Casey felt the band around her forehead tingle. A metallic taste flooded across her tongue. The sensation reminded her of the moment in the tunnels on Hosin when Xolotl reached out a tentacle to her and invited her into the mindscape – the telepathic world the Squids shared. But there were no Squids here, only Scratch and her strange device.

"I want to know about your friends in the Resistance. Where is their base? Who is their informer? When we're done with that, you can tell me all about the Bactu and this power you call *flow*."

"I won't tell you anything," Casey vowed. "I'll fight you every step of the way."

"I was hoping you'd say that," Scratch replied, hissing viciously. "It will make this much more fun." She picked up a device that looked like a virtual reality headset and slipped it over her reptilian face.

Casey felt her brain shudder as if something was invading it. Inquisitive invisible tendrils crept through the nooks and crannies of her consciousness, reaching deep into the recesses of her mind. The light shining in her eyes seemed to get brighter and brighter. Before she knew it, she was lost inside it.

18

THE MINDSCAPE 2.0

White. That was all Casey could see. A brilliant white, as spotless as clean sheets in a laundry advert. The expanse of nothingness stretched out in all directions. There were no landmarks, no features. Even the chair had vanished, releasing her from its straps. She looked down at her hands, desperate to anchor herself to something before she lost her mind. She was relieved to see they were still there.

A figure materialized in front of her.

Scratch.

"Is this the mindscape?" Casey asked, recalling the virtual world that the Squids had created with their telepathic powers. Cheeze and Fish had caused chaos in it on Hosin when they realized that they could get anything they wanted just by visualizing it. She closed her eyes and tried to imagine an energy sword filling her hand. Nothing happened.

"This isn't the Bactu's mindscape," Scratch told her. "We created this using our Arcturian technology. We made some *improvements,* too. To start with, you'll find that your user privileges have been revoked. No energy swords for you." The alien laughed at her own joke.

"Why are we here?" Casey demanded.

"To get answers to my questions."

"I've already told you, I won't give up my friends. I'd rather die than tell you what you want to know."

"Very well." Scratch nodded. "Let's play a game."

Casey blinked and found herself standing in a primary-coloured cartoon world. The transition was so abrupt it made her stomach flip. She doubled over for a moment, thinking she was about to throw up. Satisfied she wasn't about to revisit her lunch, she looked around.

She was standing on a giant red girder set against a black sky. The girder stretched in front of her across empty space. Craning her neck, she could see more girders stacked above her, each connected to the one below by blue ladders.

It was something she'd seen before. Was it from a movie or a cartoon? She gasped as the realization hit her.

It was *Donkey Kong*!

She remembered the old 8-bit video game her dad had shown her and Pete years ago. He'd told them it was a classic, one of the biggest games in video arcades in the eighties and the birthplace of Mario, the most famous video-game character ever. In the game you guided a little jumping guy with a bushy moustache up a tower of girders, scaling an unfinished skyscraper. Your goal was to rescue a kidnapped princess at the very top. To reach her you had to jump over falling barrels that rolled down along the sloping girders from the top of the screen. They were thrown by...

ROAR!

The sound shook the girders. Looking up, Casey saw a giant gorilla standing on the very top of the skyscraper. He thumped his chest angrily.

Donkey Kong! The game's princess-kidnapping villain!

The gorilla picked up a barrel from a stack beside him and threw it down towards Casey. It bounced along the sloping girders, picking up speed.

She had to move!

Casey ran to the first ladder and pulled herself up its rungs. The giant gorilla was still roaring. Beside him a girl in a pink dress was trapped, his prisoner. Her name was Pauline, Casey remembered. She was an early version of Peach, the princess for ever in need of rescue by Mario – at least until the game designers discovered girl power and gave her some much-needed backbone.

More barrels were cascading towards her. She jumped the first one as it approached, her body suspended in mid-air for a split second, just like the blocky hero in the game, and the barrel rolled underneath her. But the second barrel caught Casey by surprise, knocking her off her feet and sending her into a spin. The gorilla thumped his chest in delight.

The game reset and Casey was back at the bottom of the skyscraper again. She looked up and locked eyes with the furious gorilla. With a jolt of surprise, she realized it was actually Scratch in disguise. This wasn't a game. It was Scratch's way of getting inside her head and breaking down her mental defences. If she lost, who knew what the gorilla would take from her as his prize? She balled her hands into fists, determined not to give away the location of the Resistance or her friends.

"Think you're good at video games?" the alien hissed, speaking through the gorilla's mouth. Casey ignored the taunts and ran along the girder again. She pulled herself up the first ladder. The barrels were already rolling towards her. One burst into flames, adding further danger. She racked her brain, trying to remember what her dad had taught her about *Donkey Kong* all those years earlier.

It was, she realized, a game about timing. Jump

the barrels at the right moment and you'd stay alive. Try to push too far up the girders between each barrel's approach and you'd come unstuck. There was something else, though, Casey remembered. Something that would help you, like a power-up. She cursed herself, unable to think straight. The game's crunchy 8-bit sound effects were echoing around her, spoiling her concentration.

She raced for the ladder onto the next level, dodging a barrel as it flew past. As she did, she noticed an object hanging in mid-air above her.

The hammer!

It was the game's sole power-up, a sledgehammer that could smash every barrel. Casey ran towards it and as soon as she picked it up her body went into overdrive. Her arms lifted the hammer with superhuman strength, smashing it up and down in a blur of motion. Every barrel she encountered was obliterated on impact. The game played a celebratory snatch of music – *duh-delalala-duh-da-duh-da!* – to encourage her on.

Above her, the giant ape growled furiously. Casey tossed aside the hammer as it ran out of charge and climbed the last two girders. She ignored Pauline – that girl should save herself for once – and charged straight at Donkey Kong. She was determined to end this. Before she could reach him, the girder beneath her feet vanished and she found herself falling, falling, falling into the empty void below.

The last thing she saw was Donkey Kong beating his chest and laughing at her.

Casey fell for what seemed like an eternity. Finally, and without any warning, she landed square on her feet. The impact was smooth and seamless, like it was the most natural thing in the world. She looked around, her heart racing with fright. She was back in the white void.

She tried to remind herself that none of this was real. Nothing in this place could hurt her, at least not physically. The alien was using this strange tech to ransack her memories, searching for clues about the Resistance. She steeled herself, determined not to betray anyone. Her friends were depending on her. She couldn't fail.

"Choose another game," Scratch said, appearing in front of her, now in her true reptilian form. "Anything you like."

Casey felt her forehead throb. She sensed that Scratch was probing her mind, trying to get past her defences. She fought against it, trying not to think of anything that could help Scratch get what she wanted. She buried all thoughts of the Resistance, Haruto and the mysterious informer on the motorcycle.

Instead, she thought about her dad and about all the

games he'd shown her. She had a sudden memory of being in his study, surrounded by video-game consoles. In her mind's eye she ran her hand along the shelves full of retro games, letting her fingertips brush over the cartridges. She stopped on one and pulled it from the stack.

It was *Street Fighter II*.

Immediately, Casey's stomach flipped as the surroundings changed once again. The office vanished and she found herself on the dock of a harbour. A small steamboat bobbed in the water nearby, the deck full of spectators cheering with excitement. A girl stood on the quay wearing a blue Chinese dress. Her dark hair was tied into ox horns and she wore bangles studded with sharp spikes around her wrists. Casey recognized her as Chun-Li.

"This will be our next game," Chun-Li said, speaking with Scratch's voice.

Casey felt her body assume a fighting stance from the game. She bounced on her feet slightly, her body limber and loose. Looking down, she realized she wasn't herself any more. She had morphed into Ryu, the muscular martial arts fighter with his white karate suit and red headband. She stared at her masculine hands, callused from years of dojo training. What could she do with hands like these? She tried to remember the move set from the game. But *Street Fighter II* wasn't a game she'd ever really played. She'd always preferred shooting games to fighting ones.

"Round One! Fight!" an announcer cried. Without warning, Chun-Li flew forward, spinning through the air towards her. Casey felt the girl's boots connect with her face and she cried out in pain. This wasn't like any video game she'd played before; the blows felt real.

Casey staggered back, trying to buy herself some time. But Chun-Li was on her again. This time the Chinese girl jumped forward and turned upside down in mid-air, defying gravity as only video-game characters can. She spun through the empty air with her legs spinning above her like helicopter blades. It was her famous Spinning Bird Kick.

Casey took the whirring blows in the face one after another. She fell to the ground, stunned. It was a knockout. The first round was over. She hadn't landed a single hit against her opponent. The screen reset and the announcer's voice returned.

"Round Two! Fight!"

This time Casey was ready. She launched herself forward, letting her body move without engaging her brain. She landed a couple of punches on Chun-Li, but then the Chinese girl dropped low and swept at her ankles, trying to knock her over. Casey somersaulted backwards, feeling the raw power in Ryu's muscled body. He was built like a lump of granite, yet he moved with the grace of a ballet dancer. She threw a tight punch. Chun-Li blocked it and launched a furious kicking attack at her, her legs blurring until they looked like they were on fire. This was Chun-Li's special Lightning Kick, another of the super combos the fighters in the game had at their disposal.

Casey thought back to Brain playing *Street Fighter II* in FunZone. He'd known all the fighting combos for Ryu. If only he was here now to help her.

Chun-Li stood in front of her, waiting, a sly smile spreading over her face. Casey could feel Scratch's presence behind the fighter's avatar. The alien was clearly enjoying this. Chun-Li launched another attack, using both her hands and her feet as she rained blows down on Ryu.

Casey tried to block them while she desperately ransacked her memories of Brain's fight against Fish in FunZone. She saw him hunched over the arcade machine; the Resistance fighters crowded around as they cheered the two boys on. She remembered how the light from the screen flickered over his glasses and the intense look of concentration on his face. Brain, she realized, had found his own flow in that fight. She watched his hands moving over the controls, waggling the joystick and tapping the buttons – down, down and forward, forward and punch to release Ryu's *hadouken* energy ball.

That was it!

She jumped backwards, putting some distance between herself and Chun-Li, and planted her feet firmly on the ground. She crouched twice, moved forward twice, and then raised her hands as if to punch. As she did, she felt the energy gather inside her, rushing along her spine and then down her into her arms and hands. Her fingertips crackled.

Casey looked at Chun-Li and gestured for her to attack.

But Chun-Li didn't move.

"It's over," the Chinese girl said in Scratch's mocking voice.

"Not yet," Casey replied. The energy ball was forming between her hands. She was ready to throw it at her opponent and finish this fight for good.

"The Squids were foolish to give powers like these to a child," Scratch chided. "You are not ready for them."

Casey set her jaw hard and released the energy ball from her hands.

"*Hadouken!*" she yelled in Ryu's voice.

This would be her victory!

Before the energy ball reached its target, the

quayside suddenly vanished. Chun-Li melted into thin air like a ghost and Casey found herself back in the interrogation room, strapped to the chair, with the light shining in her face. Scratch stood over her, a sly smile playing across her lizard lips as she removed her virtual reality headset.

"Why did you stop the match?" Casey cried. "I was about to win." She felt totally cheated.

"Because you'd already lost," Scratch said, her forked tongue hissing with delight. "You told me everything I needed to know."

Casey choked, sensing she'd made a mistake.

"FunZone, the arcade machines, *Street Fighter*," the alien continued. "In your blind desire to win, your subconscious gave me all the information I wanted. I know where the Resistance are based, and I know where to find your friends. You have betrayed them."

"No!" Casey shouted, suddenly realizing what she'd done. She should never have thought of FunZone while the alien was inside her head. All her secrets – everything she'd tried to keep buried to protect the Resistance – were now in the enemy's hands.

19

HUNT 'EM DOWN, LOCK 'EM UP

The Red Caps moved at dawn. Pete watched as a bulldozer ploughed through the boarded-up hoarding of FunZone. Plasterboard and glass smashed, exposing the insides of the arcade to the light for the first time in years. Two squads of soldiers stormed in behind the bulldozer, plasma rifles at the ready. Several Resistance fighters ran for the back door, only to find their escape route blocked. The Red Caps took them down with brutal efficiency.

Once the building was secure, Pete stepped inside and looked around. The machines flashed and blinked merrily, oblivious to what had just taken place. He ran a hand over one of the cabinets. This was exactly the kind of place his dad would have loved. He pushed the thought away. Thinking about his dad made him feel sad and, if he was honest, a little ashamed.

Pete tapped his tablet and the names and mugshots of each arrestee flashed up on his screen. He was surprised to see the majority were teenagers.

"Have you found the leader?" He checked his tablet for the name. "Haruto Tanaka?"

"He's gone to ground," a Red Cap sergeant replied. "We've put out an alert for him."

Pete nodded.

"Put the rest of them in the van," he ordered.

The sergeant snapped a tight salute. "What should we do about the machines, sir?"

Pete stared at the arcade cabinets, thoughts of his dad rising to the surface again. He shook them off. It was no time to be sentimental. "Smash the place up."

As the prisoners were loaded into the waiting vans, they stared at Pete with hatred. A petite girl, whose name had flashed up as *Jude James* on Pete's tablet, broke free from the Red Caps and ran towards him.

"Traitor!" she yelled. The Red Caps reached for their shock batons, but he waved them to stand down. He approached the girl, aware that the eyes of the soldiers were on him. He couldn't show any kind of weakness. He had to play his part.

"You were at the party with Casey and the Reapers," he said. "I saw you serving drinks. Where did they go?"

"We got split up," Jude said. Her body tensed with

hatred. "How does it feel to sell out your own kind?"

"The Arcturians are here to look after us," Pete said, repeating the propaganda that was pumped out by every TV station 24/7. "They bring peace and prosperity to all."

"They're evil!" Jude exclaimed. "And you are too!" She spat at his feet and a glob of saliva hit his shoe. Pete watched as it slid off the leather.

"Take her away," he ordered the soldiers. He was glad to get away from her burning hatred.

Rounding up the rest of the Resistance took two days and two nights. The information Casey had unwittingly given Scratch allowed the Arcturians and their allies to smash open the whole network. Pete was surprised by how many hideouts there were. The group at FunZone was one of many cells. He watched as the Red Caps stormed a bakery, two abandoned tube stations on the District Line, and even a derelict tower block in Finsbury Park. He tried to imagine what it must have been like for them to hide out over the last few years. While he'd been bunking with Xander in the lap of luxury, the Resistance had lived a life of adventure and camaraderie in these makeshift bases.

He knew which one he'd have preferred.

Every time the Red Caps found a new hideout, Pete hoped they'd discover some incredible plan that the Resistance had hidden up their sleeves to end the Arcturian occupation. But there was nothing. The faces of the young Resistance fighters being led out to the police vans said it all. They looked utterly defeated. In a day or so, when the Red Eyes activated the array, it really would all be over. There would be no one left to stop the aliens from getting what they wanted.

No one at all ... except him.

When the last hideout had been shut down, Pete tapped at his tablet. He scrolled through the list of Resistance fighters, looking at their faces one by one. A soldier appeared beside him and cleared his throat. "The last of the prisoners have been secured. Are we done now, sir?"

"Not yet," Pete told him. "We have one more stop to make."

They arrived at the old Saudi ambassador's mansion just before midnight. Scratch was already on the gravel driveway, waiting patiently. Pete suspected that she was looking forward to this moment even more than he was.

"Excellent work, Peter," she said. "The Resistance is finished."

"We're still searching for the rest of the Reapers," Pete explained, passing her his tablet so she could see the prisoner list for herself. "The boy Haruto, too."

"My forces have a lead on them," the alien said,

her face once again obscured by her hood. "They used Commander Deacon's passkey to ransack a supply depot in the east of the city last night. Weapons were stolen."

Pete tried hard not to let his emotions show at this news. "That's worrying," he remarked.

"They won't evade us for long, not without their *Cay-See*," Scratch hissed.

Pete's chest tightened in disgust. These were his friends she was talking about. His sister, too. Didn't the alien realize what that meant to him? Or was she convinced that he had totally swapped sides?

"I am impressed by your work, Peter," the alien said.

"I can't take the credit," Pete replied. "Your suspicions about the informer were correct, Overseer."

"Who confirmed it?"

"A girl called Jude James. She said she'd seen him with Haruto several times." Pete swallowed hard. He'd never thought of himself as a very good liar. But Scratch nodded, satisfied.

There was a shout at the front door as two Red Caps pushed past the butler and burst into the lavish hallway. They ignored the old man's protestations and marched upstairs. A moment later they returned with Xander, bleary-eyed and wearing nothing but his boxers and a T-shirt. Lisa ran behind him in a bathrobe, tears running down her face.

"Don't you know who I am?" the YouTuber shouted at the soldiers as they dragged him outside. "I'll have all your caps for this!" His face lit up when he saw Pete and Scratch on the driveway. "Pete!" he yelled. "Thank god you're here! They're saying I'm some kind of informer... Is this a joke?" He looked around. "Is it a prank? For TV? Where are you hiding the cameras?"

"No cameras tonight," Scratch hissed in a low, menacing voice. "Maybe never again. We have suspected there was a spy feeding information to the Resistance for a long time. Now we've finally found you."

"No!" Xander cried. "You're making a mistake. I'm a dealmaker, not a blabbermouth!"

The alien regarded him a moment from beneath her hood. Xander's face shifted from hope to despair. He looked ridiculous standing there in his underwear, his floppy fringe in his eyes, shivering in the cold night air.

"Take him away," Scratch said, clicking her talons at the Red Caps. They fitted a shock shackle around the YouTuber's neck.

"What will happen to him, Overseer?" Pete asked, feeling a sudden pang of guilt. He didn't want to see Xander harmed, even though he knew that he had to get him out of the way to save himself. Was this what it felt like to be ruthless, he wondered? He wasn't sure he liked it.

"He'll be sent to join the work crews like every spy and traitor," Scratch told him.

They watched as the Red Caps led Xander towards the prisoner transport. He struggled against them, unable to believe his predicament. Lisa stood nearby, sobbing. Pete was glad she wasn't being arrested too.

The YouTuber caught Pete's eye as he was shoved into the back of the van. "Pete!" Xander cried. "You've got to help me! Tell them I'd never do anything that wasn't for the glory of Arcturia!"

Pete looked at the teenager a moment. He thought about how the YouTuber had convinced him to abandon his friends and work with the aliens; how he'd encouraged him to sell out his sister; and how he'd preyed on his fears and manipulated him. Xander wasn't his friend. He didn't care for anyone but himself.

"Please," Xander begged. "This isn't right. TELL THEM! They need me. YOU need me!"

Pete shook his head. He was done with Xander. "Try not to worry," he told the YouTuber. "It's for the win." Then he crossed his index fingers into an "X".

Xander's face crumpled in shock and surprise as he realized Pete's betrayal. The Red Caps led him away.

Pete felt a rush of relief. The apprentice had outwitted the master.

He was finally free.

Scratch's scaly arm snaked across his shoulders. He froze.

"So, Peter," the alien hissed, "now that we have found the informer, the time has come for you to step up. Tomorrow you will help me unleash the array."

"For the glory of Arcturia," Pete said with passion.

If he was going to see his plan through to the end, he knew he would have to be convincing.

20

PRISONER CELL BLOCK H

"They're saying they've busted the whole network wide open."

"I heard they've made a hundred arrests across London, alone."

From her cell, Casey strained to hear the voices of the guards outside. She'd discovered that if she kept her ear against the grille over the viewing slit in the door she could just about follow their conversations.

There were two sets of guards working in shifts. The chattiest were called Graham and Maggie. Graham was in his thirties and had two young kids. He talked about how much he missed the Premier League since the Red Eyes had arrived and complained about how little sleep he got because of his new baby. He'd been a cop before the invasion and he liked to say that working for the Red Eyes was a case of "meet the new boss, same as the old boss". Casey sensed he said it to convince himself that he didn't need to feel guilty. He was firm but fair and would sometimes chat to the prisoners. Mostly about his new baby.

Maggie was older, twice divorced, and lived with a tabby cat that had a habit of bringing her dead sparrows. She thought this was "cute". She'd been a customer services manager in a call centre before the invasion and she had joined the Red Caps when the Arcturians took over. Her favourite pastime was shouting abuse at the prisoners. She liked to bang on the cell doors as loudly as possible during the night to wake everyone up. Casey wondered if she was taking her revenge for all the years she'd spent having angry customers shouting down the phone at her.

Listening to the guards' chat was the only thing Casey had to pass the time. It kept her mind active, although the news she overheard frequently made her despair. Reports were coming in that the Resistance had been rounded up in a city-wide sweep. Graham and Maggie talked in excited tones whenever another Resistance cell was discovered and broken up.

Casey strained to hear news of the Ghost Reapers and, most of all, her mum, but nobody mentioned them. Her mum was being held under house arrest, Pete had said. But she had no idea where the Reapers were. They might still be on the run – or maybe they had all gone back to their families. She wouldn't blame them if they had.

Not that it really mattered, either way. She knew deep down that the Arcturians had won. They'd taken over the planet. They'd corrupted the politicians and billionaires with promises of riches and prosperity. They'd found every single piece of the array. And now, on the cusp of victory, they'd destroyed the only group that had a chance of stopping them.

She curled up on her bed and shivered, even though she wasn't cold. The black metal band around her forehead was tight and painful. She knew it was blocking her powers. Without it she would have ripped the cell door off its hinges by now.

The viewing slot in the cell door opened. Maggie's eyes, lined by thick mascara, stared in.

"Chow time!"

She shoved a tray of food through the serving hatch. Casey took it. The tray was split into three sections with a different coloured paste in each. Casey grimaced. She'd give anything for a proper meal. "Please put any complaints in writing to the Arcturians," Maggie laughed, slamming the hatch on her.

Casey sat on the edge of her bunk and spooned some brown paste into her mouth. It tasted of meat, although what kind of meat exactly she couldn't say. She swallowed it mechanically, then spooned up some of the green paste beside it. This tasted vaguely of boiled cabbage. Not vaguely enough for her liking.

She was about to swallow when her teeth crunched down on something unexpectedly hard. She spat the object into her hand. It was a pharmaceutical pill, one of those red-and-white capsules with powder inside. Casey wiped the paste off it and examined it with her fingertips, wondering what it was doing in her food. Was Maggie trying to poison her? It didn't seem likely. If the invaders wanted Casey dead, they had a million better ways of bumping her off.

Intrigued, she turned her back to the surveillance camera on the ceiling and prised the capsule apart with her fingertips. A tiny scroll of tightly wound paper fell out. She wiped her fingers on her trousers before unrolling it. There were words printed on it, but in a font so small she had to squint to read them:

Escape tonight.
Be ready.
Don't ask questions.
A friend.

She stared at the paper, uncertain. Was this a trap?

Or was someone really trying to rescue her? Maybe the Reapers had found where she was being held. She imagined Brain devising a plan, pushing his glasses up his nose, carefully explaining things to his teammates and sighing at Elite's terrible rapping. Cheeze finding a way to hack the security cameras. Fish complaining as he was forced to wear a Red Cap uniform as a disguise...

She was being ridiculous. There was no way her friends could get her out of this cell. They'd need passes, security clearances and weapons. Maybe if the Resistance was still up and running, Haruto and Jude could have used their network to pull some strings. But that was all over now.

Someone had put the note in her paste, though. Someone who was trying to get a message to her. Someone who claimed to be a friend. She sighed and reread it, imprinting the words in her memory. Then she rubbed the paper between her fingers until it disintegrated. She'd just have to wait and see what happened.

She didn't mean to fall asleep, but it was hard to stay awake when there was nothing to do. She woke after what felt like a couple of hours, disturbed by the sound of her cell door opening. It took her a moment to realize that this wasn't a normal inspection. Maggie hadn't opened the viewing slot and barked instructions like she usually did.

Casey sat up, rubbing the sleep from her eyes quickly so she'd be ready for whatever was about to happen. Part of her still didn't believe the note. It felt like it might be a cruel trick, although she wasn't sure what anyone would hope to gain from it. Scratch had ransacked her brain already, taking everything useful. There was nothing left for Casey to give.

It *had* to be a rescue.

Her heart sank when she saw the figure standing in the doorway. They were dressed in black like a Red Cap, although instead of the customary red beret they wore a black motorcycle helmet. The visor, tinted and impossible to see through, was down obscuring their face. She couldn't even tell if they were male or female.

The motorcyclist stared at her a moment, head on one side. Casey took the opportunity to stand up. If she was going to have to fight, at least she'd be on her feet. As she did, she realized she'd seen this figure before. This was the informer Haruto had spoken to before the party.

"You're here to help me?" Casey asked cautiously.

The motorcyclist nodded and beckoned her to step forward. Casey paused, weighing up her options. If this was a trick it was pretty elaborate. She decided to go with it and see what happened.

They slipped out of the cell together, pulling the door shut without making a sound. Graham and Maggie were in their booth at the far end of the corridor. Graham was watching an old football match he'd recorded before the invasion.

As they crept closer to the booth, Casey saw that both guards were slumped in their chairs fast asleep. A flask of coffee and a box of doughnuts sat open beside them.

"Drugged?" Casey whispered.

Her silent rescuer ignored her, too busy punching numbers into the security door at the end of cell block. Casey wondered where they'd got the codes from. She guessed they must have access to the Red Caps' systems. She tensed, uncertain what that meant.

The security door opened into the police station's custody suite. Two Red Caps were at the booking-in desk, dealing with an unruly prisoner. A couple more officers were in the locker room, getting changed into their uniforms for the start of their shift.

The motorcyclist waited until no one was looking and then stepped out and signalled Casey to follow. Together they hurried down a corridor towards another security door. This one led into the police station's reception area. A Red Cap sat behind a reception counter with a Perspex screen. Opposite him was a set of sliding doors that led out onto the street. Casey felt a thrill of elation. She was only twenty or so steps away from freedom. Could it really be that easy?

They crossed the reception area at a brisk pace, walking confidently. They'd just made it to the doors when the Red Cap behind the desk suddenly looked up.

"Hey!" he cried, noticing the band around Casey's head. "What's going on?"

The motorcyclist shoved Casey through the doors and out into the night air. An alarm began to sound in the police station. They hurried down the building's front steps onto the street. The motorcyclist's bike was parked by the kerb at the bottom of the steps. It was sleek and black and almost invisible in the darkness. Its owner reached inside the saddlebags.

Casey hoped they were grabbing a weapon.

"Stop right there!" a Red Cap shouted from the steps of the police station. He sounded like he was auditioning to be an extra in a cheap straight-to-Netflix movie. He drew a plasma pistol, ready to fire. Three more soldiers joined him on the steps.

The motorcyclist took their hand from the saddlebag. It was empty.

"Don't you have a gun?" Casey asked, panicking.

"Just do what I do," the motorcyclist instructed

her. It was the first time they'd spoken and Casey still wasn't sure if the muffled voice that came from inside the helmet belonged to a boy or a girl.

"Back away from the bike," the Red Caps ordered, coming down the steps towards them. Casey and her rescuer raised their hands in the air. The motorcyclist took a step backwards, and then another and another. Casey matched them step for step, wondering what was going on. The Red Caps approached them, moving around the motorbike. Casey wondered if she should try and make a run for it, but something about the motorcyclist's body language made her hesitate. They were unfazed. Like they knew something no one else did.

"Get down on your knees," a Red Cap ordered.

Casey looked at the motorcyclist, uncertain what to do. They didn't move.

"Wait for it," they whispered. "Just another second…"

The Red Cap was annoyed by their failure to comply. "I said, get down on the—"

There was a thud and then a hiss as something detonated inside the motorcycle's saddlebags. A thick plume of grey smoke filled the air, clouding the Red Caps' vision.

"Run!" Casey's rescuer yelled, grabbing her hand.

They pulled her sideways across the street, their escape covered by the smoke grenade. The Red Caps fired blindly into the billowing clouds, unable to find their targets.

Casey and her rescuer sprinted to the junction down the street. As they got there a Luton van appeared. Casey recognized it, even before she saw the words CLEAN ME! written in the grime along its side. The vehicle braked and swerved in front of them, almost toppling over.

"Get in!" yelled Elite from the driver's seat, Brain beside him.

Casey didn't need to be told twice. She jumped in the back. The motorcyclist climbed in next to her, helped in by Fish and Cheeze. The van tore off down the street.

"Guys!" Casey cried. "I can't believe you rescued me! Thank you!"

"Don't thank us," Cheeze said, nodding at the motorcyclist. "He's your saviour."

Casey stared in amazement as the black-clad figure lifted the visor on their helmet.

"Hi, sis."

21

UNDER THE RADAR

The van pulled up in the shadow of the Westway flyover. Elite had twisted and turned through the city streets at top speed, avoiding being tracked with a skill behind the wheel that even Brain had to begrudgingly admire. The Reapers knew that they couldn't stay ahead of the Red Caps for ever, though, especially not when the night-time streets were so quiet. Hiding out until daylight seemed like the safest option. They would just have to hope that the flyover would keep the van from being spotted by any Arcturian drones flying overhead.

The waste ground beneath the flyover was littered with oil drums, weeds and a few shacks made out of wooden pallets and sheets of plastic. A group of homeless citizens inhabited the makeshift structures, eking out a precarious existence. Across the junction a huge electronic display board was mounted on the side of an abandoned office block. It pumped out a non-stop barrage of Arcturian propaganda.

No one bothered the Reapers as they warmed themselves beside a fire lit inside a scavenged oil drum. The people who lived here looked downtrodden, miserable and defeated. Not even the sight of Cheeze's hoverchair aroused more than a cursory glance.

As the team regrouped, Cheeze examined the band around Casey's forehead.

"It's metal, I think," he said, his fingers running over the device, intrigued. "But not like anything I've seen before. It must be some alien alloy."

"All I want to know is how to get it off," Casey told him. Using a small screwdriver from the pouch on the side of his hoverchair, Cheeze tried to open up the control box attached to the band.

"Ow!" Casey complained, feeling her head being squeezed.

"It's designed to tighten if it's interfered with," Pete told them. "You'll need to short circuit it. Fry the circuit board before it gets a chance to react."

Cheeze nodded, already reaching back into his toolkit for his cordless soldering iron. "A bit of heat should do it."

As Cheeze prepped the soldering iron, Casey regarded her brother across the oil barrel. The flicker of the fire played over his face. She didn't quite know where to begin.

"So," she finally said. "You were the informer? You were helping the Resistance all along? Why?"

"I was trying to do some good," Pete mumbled, shifting uncomfortably as the others turned to look at him. "I thought I could make a difference."

Casey stared at him, taking in his new maturity. There was still something of her little brother in his mannerisms, she realized.

"Tell me what happened," she whispered, ready to hear him out. "Start at the beginning."

"We should be careful what we say," Brain warned with a careful nod towards the homeless citizens near by.

"No one's going to bother you here," a bearded man in a lumberjack shirt growled as he tossed firewood into the barrel. "We ain't fans of the Arcturians." He looked at Pete a moment, perhaps recognizing his face from the TV broadcasts. The boy shrank into the shadows until the man moved on.

"You need to tell us what's been going on," Casey told her brother. "We need to know where we stand."

Pete kept his eyes on the fire. "I know I messed up," he said. "I've had four years to think about what I should and shouldn't have done. When I left you on

Hosin, I just wanted to get home. I was so scared. Then Xander said he could make a deal that would get us back and..." His voice trailed off and he fell silent.

"But why did you keep helping the Red Eyes once you got back to Earth?" Casey demanded.

"You think I had a choice?" Pete asked, raising his voice. "If I didn't help them they would have used their mind-control devices on me. I'm not brave like you, Casey. I'm a coward."

Brain blew out his cheeks. "Sometimes all it takes for evil to triumph is for good people to do nothing."

"I thought I *was* one of the good people," Pete said, flinching at the implication of Brain's words. "I mean, I wasn't like Xander. I didn't help them because I wanted to be rich or famous. I did it to survive."

Casey remembered what Mum had said about the invasion.

That's all any of us are doing ... surviving.

"Why didn't you just tell them everything, then?" Casey asked, perplexed. "Why all the big drama about doing research to find each piece of the array, when you knew where they all were right from the beginning?"

Pete's face clouded. "I was stalling for time! I thought if I kept stringing them along, giving them the info bit by bit, someone would eventually fight back. But no one did. Then I heard about the Resistance. I thought they might have a chance of stopping the Arcturians. I didn't realize they were mostly kids. Just like me."

"Just like all of us, bruv," Elite chipped in.

Casey stared into the flames. A piece of wood popped and crackled. It felt like Pete had betrayed everything she believed in, every value they'd shared.

"What would Dad say if he was here?"

As soon as the words were out of her mouth, she knew it was a low blow. But she couldn't find it in herself to take it back. Without a word, Pete turned on his heel and vanished into the shadows.

The Ghost Reapers stood in silence a moment, uncomfortable.

"He made a mistake," Cheeze told her quietly. "No one's saying you have to forgive him, but you don't have to keep punishing him either." He paused, waiting for her to respond. "You know, the only reason we got away from the Arcturians is because he helped us."

"I got you out of the ballroom," Casey replied, irritated. "I blew out the windows. I even let myself be captured so you could get away."

"No," Cheeze said, "I'm talking about what happened afterwards."

"What do you mean?"

"After we left you, we headed back to FunZone to regroup. Haruto convinced us to hit the supply depot and grab the weapons using Commander Deacon's passkey. While we were gone, though, the Red Eyes raided FunZone. Pete warned us it was going down. If he hadn't, we would have been captured with Jude and the others. He saved us."

"Where *is* Haruto?" Casey asked, looking around the group.

"As soon as he heard FunZone was toast, he ditched us," Cheeze explained. "He knew we didn't have the manpower to take down the *Blocka* servers any more. The whole plan fell apart."

Casey thought about how volatile Haruto was. She knew nothing good could come of this. "What's he going to do?"

"Dude tooled up with a sniper rifle from the supply depot," Elite told her. "I reckon he's gonna go after the emperor. Boom! Headshot."

Casey fell silent and watched the flames licking the night air. Frustrated by her lack of response, Cheeze spun his hoverchair around and went in search of Pete. The rest of the Reapers followed him, leaving Casey to her thoughts.

She watched the fire splutter. Pete *had* tried to help the Resistance, she realized. He'd done everything he could to try and stop the Red Eyes from getting what they wanted. Maybe Cheeze was right, that had taken courage. Who was she to judge him, anyway? She'd given Scratch everything the Arcturians needed to smash the Resistance's network, including FunZone's location. She sighed, depressed. This wasn't a video game where you could reload your game and make different choices. In real life every decision was a permanent one. You just had to make the best of them and learn from your mistakes.

Casey pulled herself away from the fire and headed over to where Pete was talking with the rest of the Reapers. He started when he saw her, expecting another barrage of aggro. But Casey just grabbed him and hugged him tight. They stood there a moment, holding one another. It was the longest she could ever remember hugging her brother.

"I'm sorry," he whispered.

"I'm sorry too. Things were never meant to get this messed up."

After a few moments, Pete pulled himself free of Casey's embrace and wiped his eyes, embarrassed in front of the other boys.

"What happens now?" he asked, looking at his sister.

"You need to tell us everything you know about the final piece of the array," Casey said. "And then we need to work out how to stop the Red Eyes from activating it."

Pete nodded. "They found it a few days ago," he

explained. "They've got a team of hackers working around the clock trying to break the security code on it so they can activate it. They're using crowdsourced data from *Blocka*."

Brain and Cheeze exchanged a satisfied smile at this. Their theory about the game had been right.

"What happens when they activate it?" Fish asked Pete.

"They're going to turn it into a weapon. Scratch said it would be so powerful they could take over the universe with it. Like the Death Star, I guess. But I don't really know the details. Scratch never liked talking about it, at least not with me."

"So, if the emperor gets hold of this thing he becomes the Arcturian version of Darth Vader?" Elite asked.

"Palpatine," Brain corrected him. "Darth Vader's more like, I dunno, Scratch."

Cheeze shook his head. "Scratch would be Kylo Ren. He's a better character than Vader anyway."

"You can't compare Kylo with Vader, bruv," Elite protested. "Kylo's a whiny brat."

"He's not whiny. He's conflicted ... complicated."

"He has a tantrum every five minutes!"

"You're all wrong," Fish chipped in. "If the Red Eyes get the array they'll turn into the evillest character in the whole *Star Wars* universe ... Jar Jar Binks."

His teammates stared at him, incredulous.

"You're out of your mind, bruv!"

"I'm telling you: Jar Jar is a Sith Lord on the down-low," Fish said defensively. "I watched a YouTube video about it."

"And I watched a YouTube video about boys growing breasts after drinking soya milk," said Brain. "It didn't mean I believed it."

"Guys! This isn't helping!" Casey warned. She knew if they started nerding out on *Star Wars* fan theories, they'd never stop the Red Eyes. The boys clammed up, coming back to their senses. "Listen," Casey said. "The Squids said the array was originally a communications device."

"What, like E.T. phone home?" Elite grinned, holding his hand to his ear like a phone. "Can we call someone to come save us?"

"Just don't call Jar Jar," Cheeze muttered.

"Xolotl told me it could reach out across the universe to other caretaker races just like them," Casey continued. "Maybe we can use it to get help? Ask someone to come and save us?"

She glanced over at the huge advertising screen. It was playing footage from the dig site at Stonehenge. Diggers and cranes and hundreds of labourers worked to excavate the enormous Squid structure from beneath the famous standing stones. A scrolling banner at the bottom of the screen read: *Final piece of the array discovered. Arcturian victory imminent…*

Pete cleared his throat. "Private Ross told me that ship was the control centre for the whole thing. If they can power it up, it'll link up all the other pieces of the array across the globe. It's why I left it until last."

Casey stared at the screen. The object *did* look like a spaceship. Maybe it was one of the ships the Squids had used when they first visited Earth millennia before. She wished Xolotl was here to tell them what to do. But it was only her, her brother and the Reapers. Just like it had been at the very beginning.

She squared her shoulders, realizing what that meant. They had started this and now they had to finish it, too.

"We need to get to Stonehenge," she said decisively. "And fast."

22

THREE LEGS GOOD, FOUR WHEELS BAD

Casey and the boys continued their journey just after dawn. Although the Reapers had snatched a couple of hours' sleep under the flyover, they were all yawning. The constant stress of being on the run was exhausting.

Their route took them along one of the main arterial roads out of London, passing the West Point shopping centre where they had first met. Casey stared in silence at the enormous building, thinking of everything that had happened since the eSports tournament and the arrival of the aliens. She tried to imagine how the future might look if they succeeded in stopping the invaders. She had no idea if the Earth could pull itself back together after everything that had happened. It was so changed, so broken.

The city was quiet, the streets deserted. They spotted the odd drone going about its business and prayed their van would pass unnoticed. It was exactly the same as the vehicles that transported goods up and down the motorways for the Arcturians, which helped. They just needed to avoid any patrols or checkpoints, since they didn't have any paperwork.

They were on the outskirts of the city when they realized there might be a problem. It began with a heavy thudding noise. At first Casey thought it was the engine failing. But the noise grew louder and more insistent, until it was too loud to be mistaken for the vehicle. Elite, behind the steering wheel, checked his mirrors with a frown and craned his neck to look up into the sky through the windscreen. It wasn't until they climbed the ramp to the top of the expressway that they saw the source of the noise.

"Goliath!" Brain yelled.

Up ahead, a giant three-legged walking machine straddled the dual carriageway. Its cannons turned towards the van as it approached. The Reapers stared through the windscreen at the machine, awed into silence by its size. Brain was the first one to speak.

"Drive," he yelled, shaking Elite's shoulder. "The moment that thing realizes we're not supposed to be out here, we'll be sitting ducks!"

Elite swerved down a slip road and tried to vanish between the rows of identical suburban houses on the outskirts of the city. The Goliath was instantly on them, its hydraulics whining as its pilot came after them in pursuit. The machine moved quickly and methodically with the darting menace of a praying mantis.

"Where do I go?" Elite shouted.

"There!" Brain shouted, seeing the entrance to a multi-storey car park across the street. "Lose it inside the car park."

The van accelerated and smashed through the barrier. There was no time to take a ticket. Elite gunned the engine and raced up the ramp onto the first level, barrelling around the corner with a screech of rubber. The place was abandoned, a couple of rusting cars dotted here and there. Petrol was in such short supply since the invasion that no one drove any more. The building itself was intact, though, a big slab of concrete and steel that might be enough to keep the Goliath at bay while they worked out what to do.

As Elite headed towards the next level, the Goliath circled the building, attempting to locate them from the outside. They could see its body bobbing up and down on its stilt-like legs as the pilot tried to spot them through the gaps between the levels.

Frustrated by this game of cat and mouse, the Goliath took a step backwards and the pilot opened up with the machine's plasma cannons. Huge sections of the car park were blown away as it blasted the building.

"It's trying to dig us out!" Elite shouted and swerved up the next ramp to get away from the barrage of deadly fire.

"How tall is this car park?" Brain asked, suddenly concerned.

"It said seven floors," Elite replied.

"How many have we done so far?"

"Dunno. I'm driving not counting!"

"Sooner or later, we're going to run out of levels," Brain muttered.

"Then what?" Pete asked from the back.

"Then we run out of levels, bruv," Elite said through gritted teeth.

"Can we get off the roof somehow?" Fish asked.

"Yeah, we can take the helicopter that's waiting for us up there," Cheeze said sarcastically.

"*Really?*" Fish replied, his eyes widening.

"Sure, I just need to call them…" Cheeze held his mobile to his ear. "Hello, is that the chopper pilot? We're coming in hot. Be ready for dustoff."

"Oh, I thought you were being serious!" Fish said with a scowl as he realized the joke was on him.

With a bump and a scrape, the van burst onto the open roof terrace at the top of the building. There was no waiting chopper. In fact, short of driving straight off the roof, there was nowhere to go. Elite slammed on the brakes as the Goliath reared above them.

"What do I do?" he asked, unable to take his eyes off the machine's enormous guns.

"Stay here," Casey said and jumped out of the cab. She ignored the concerned shouts of the boys and stepped in front of the van, placing herself between it and the enormous machine that towered above them. The huge metal contraption made her feel small and insignificant.

"Casey, get back in the van!" Brain yelled, sticking his head out of the passenger window. She ignored her friend, her mind racing. She thought of the Squid powers in *SkyWake*. What would they use on something as big as this? Psi-Blast? Telekinesis? Neither seemed strong enough to stop the Goliath. It was something new. Something that hadn't been in the game. Something the Arcturians had built since coming to Earth. She didn't know how to counter it.

She stared up into the cockpit, trying to imagine the Red Eye pilot inside the machine looking down at her. Did it make him feel powerful being in charge of something this big? He could crush her like a bug with just a flick of his controls if he wanted to.

She stopped.

That was it!

She didn't have to stop the Goliath, just the Red Eye who was operating it. She remembered how the Squids had fought their enemies in the tunnels under Hosin, reaching into their minds to confuse them. Could she do that too?

The hairs on the back of her neck began to tingle as the power coursed through her body. She felt the sensation of flow rising within her. She didn't even notice as the Goliath unleashed a cable from its undercarriage towards her.

Standing there, lost in a trance, Casey felt her mind reach outwards in a way she'd never experienced before. It was as if it was scanning the empty air, like a radio tuner searching for a broadcast signal.

Suddenly, she heard the thoughts of the Arcturian pilot. She entered his head, seeing everything through his eyes. She saw his gloved hands moving over the Goliath's controls. She saw the monitors banked around the cockpit streaming information. Finally, she saw herself on the other side of the cockpit window, standing on the roof of the car park looking up at the Goliath. It made her head spin.

As the cable from the Goliath's body prepared to wrap itself around her, Casey unleashed her power. In *SkyWake* it was known as Confusion, a special Squid ability that could temporarily invert an Arcturian player's controls. Up suddenly became down and right became left, and your fire button made you do a silly emote instead of blasting your enemies. Confusion could render Red Eye players powerless and before they knew what was happening, it was Game Over.

Here, in real life, Casey felt the pilot gasp as his mind was turned upside down. He panicked, struggling to understand what was happening. He reached for the trigger on his joystick, ready to open fire. But his hand moved in the opposite direction. He tried to look right, but his head turned left. Everything was topsy-turvy. The more he tried to fight it, the more confused he became.

Inside the van, the Reapers watched as Casey stood frozen on the roof with her hands outstretched. She looked like she was deep in a dream. The cable from the Goliath had fallen, lifeless, on the ground in front of her – although whether it was a mechanical failure or Casey's power wasn't clear. The only thing that moved was her hair. It flapped around her face, even though there was no breeze. The blue streak that ran through it flowed like a waterfall, lit up by whatever strange power was coursing through her body.

"What's happening?" Elite yelled from behind the steering wheel in the van.

"Reverse," Brain whispered.

"What?"

"Reverse now! Quick!"

Elite shunted the van backwards. A second later there was a groan of hydraulics and the Goliath stumbled, as if suddenly unsteady on its feet.

"GO!" Brain yelled. Elite pressed his foot down on the accelerator and the van slammed back down the ramp to the level below.

As the Goliath stumbled, Casey felt the pilot's panic. Perhaps with enough time he could have figured out how to counter her attack, swapping his movements around like some *SkyWake* players managed to when confused by their Squid enemies. But, with an enormous machine in his control, his fear got the better of him and the Goliath lost its balance.

"Timber!" Fish yelled, looking through the windscreen in horror. "It's coming down!"

The van reversed onto the lower level just as the Goliath collapsed onto the roof of the car park with an almighty crash. A cloud of dust and debris engulfed it.

Pete was the first to jump out, the others quickly following. He ran up the ramp, now jammed with rubble, and squeezed through onto the roof level.

"Casey!" he yelled in panic. "Casey!"

He found his sister lying in a crumpled heap beneath the Goliath's fallen body. She was, by some miracle or some incredible power, unscathed.

"Help me!" Pete cried, running over to her and pulling her free of the wreckage.

"I'm OK," she murmured weakly.

"That was intense," Cheeze said, helping Casey to her feet. "I thought you were a goner."

Casey stumbled and leaned into Pete for support.

"What's wrong?" Pete asked. "Are you hurt?"

"It's nothing…" Casey muttered as her legs buckled underneath her.

"Whoa!" Pete cried, catching her. With Elite's help he sat her down on a broken block of concrete. She was pale and out of breath. Her whole body was trembling.

"Whatever that Squid magic is, it ain't doing nothing for your health," Elite told her. "Hey, Brainiac, get over here!"

The team medic ran over. He knelt down beside Casey and took her wrist in his hand. His eyes got a little bigger behind his lenses. "Her heart's hammering like a pneumatic drill."

"And she looks as pale as a ghost that's just seen a ghost," Fish added.

"I think I pushed myself too far," Casey murmured. "These powers … they're too much for just one person."

"We have to get her to a hospital or something," Cheeze said, fretting. "She needs to be checked out."

"No, we don't have time," Casey said, shaking her

head. "Just get me to Stonehenge so we can finish this." Brain went to say something and then thought better of it. Casey was grateful to him for holding his tongue.

"Everyone back in the van," Elite ordered, waving the rest of them inside. "It's a miracle the hunk of junk is still in one piece."

Cheeze looked over at the downed Goliath.

"Maybe we're being too hasty," he said tentatively. "If we're going into the lion's den, we need to look like a lion not a gazelle."

"What are you saying, bruv?" Elite demanded.

"I think it's time we got ourselves a new ride…"

23

WONDERS OF THE ANCIENT WORLD

The Goliath strode across the fields with long, loping steps. From the cockpit Casey couldn't fail to be astonished by both its speed and its height. Sitting in the co-pilot seat, she watched as Cheeze steered it, his confidence growing with each new step.

The ride had been unsteady at first. Cheeze struggled to get the Goliath back on its feet, cursing as he fought the joystick. The Goliath stumbled left and right above the ruined car park and, more than once, Casey thought they were going to topple back over. The rest of the Reapers, watching from the car park rooftop next to the still unconscious body of the Red Eye pilot, looked on in horror. They'd all wanted to ride in the machine at first. But now that they saw how dangerous it was, they were glad to get back in the van.

By the time Cheeze got the Goliath out of London,

though, he had pretty much mastered the controls. He guided it alongside the motorway with giant steps while keeping an eye out for the electricity pylons that ran across the fields like enormous tripwires. Casey had stashed Cheeze's hoverchair in the Goliath's small cargo bay when they boarded. Yet, judging by how much he was enjoying this new ride, she wasn't sure he'd ever want it again.

"How long until we're there?" she asked, trying to make sense of the Arcturian display screens in the cockpit. The inside of the Goliath was like a fighter jet. Dials and gauges and monitors spewed out information. A joystick was mounted on either side of the pilot's seat, one for each hand. One stick controlled the Goliath's movement, the other the weapons systems.

"Not much further," Cheeze told her. "It would be quicker if we let her rip, but they can barely keep up as it is." He nodded at the Reapers' van on the motorway below them. It was already going at full speed, the exhaust coughing out black smoke. Cheeze looked over his shoulder at her. "How are you feeling?" he asked, concerned.

"Better," Casey lied. She felt weary and spaced out from fighting the Goliath. Using Confusion had taken its toll on her too.

"It's not down to you to save the world, you know,"

Cheeze said, keeping his eyes on the controls. Not for the first time she realized how lucky she was that he was part of the team. His compassion and calm gave her strength. If Brain was the smarts of the group, Cheeze was its heart. "You do know that, right?"

"Yes." Casey nodded.

"Really?"

"No," she confessed. "It feels like it's all on me. The Squids chose me. They gave me these powers that I barely know how to use and now I'm supposed to save the world with them. It's all too much."

"You make it sound like a curse, not a gift," Cheeze chided.

"That's how it feels. I never asked for any of this. I just went to the shopping centre to play video games. Now I'm the one responsible for stopping the Red Eyes." She took a deep breath. "Do you know how Scratch discovered FunZone?" she asked. "It was because I let it slip when she interrogated me. Don't you see? I'm not perfect. I make mistakes too."

Cheeze turned the Goliath sideways to avoid a copse of trees.

"We wouldn't have got this far without you, Casey," he told her, keeping his eyes on the controls. "I think you're a hero. Or a heroine. Or whatever the right non-gendered word is." He looked up at her reflection in the cockpit window shyly. She sensed he was trying to tell her how he felt about her – how he *really* felt – but she couldn't deal with that right now.

"Maybe being a hero is different in real life," Casey replied. "In stories you know the heroes won't really fail. Luke Skywalker's never going to miss his shot to blow up the Death Star, right? Stories always work out. Real life is different."

"You don't have to do this on your own. We're going to find the Squid spaceship together. We're going to stop the Red Eyes from activating the array together, too. You and me, and the rest of the Reapers and Pete. It's like *SkyWake*. You choose your role: assault, medic, sniper, tank, hacker. You can't play all of them all at once."

Casey nodded, but Cheeze could see she wasn't convinced.

"You have to let us help you," he continued, "because we've got your back. Most of all, *I've* got your back. I'm not going to let anything bad happen to you, because I—"

An alert cut him off in mid-sentence. The Goliath's screens lit up. Out of the cockpit window Casey saw three more vehicles just like theirs on the horizon. They stood on guard duty around Stonehenge, their metal chassis reflecting the morning sun. Beneath them, laid out in the middle of the rolling countryside, was the ancient archaeological site with its famous stone circle.

The site was a hive of alien activity. A huge pit had been dug around the excavated Squid spaceship. It was surrounded by construction vehicles, portacabins and tents. Arcturian digging equipment removed the dirt, but the sensitive work around the edges of the ship was done by hand to ensure no one damaged the precious vessel.

The Red Eyes had left the standing stones untouched. They sat on a circle of grass and soil on top of the enormous spaceship's hull. Casey guessed that the Arcturians were concerned that these ancient rocks might be important and didn't dare destroy them just in case. The aliens had waited so long to get hold of the array they wouldn't risk anything going wrong.

Casey thought back to what she'd learned about Stonehenge at school. The site was one of the seven wonders of the ancient world. Long ago, people thought the stones were the work of a giant, or a wizard like Merlin. Archaeologists had debunked those crazy theories over the years, yet the purpose of the stone circle remained a mystery. Some thought it could be an ancient computer used to chart the movement of the stars; others thought it was a temple where the sick and injured came to be healed.

She tried to imagine Xolotl and the Squids arriving

here, millennia ago. They had come to encourage mankind and help the human race develop. Did they build Stonehenge with their psi-powers? Lifting those lumps of rock would be easy for them. Or had it been constructed after they'd left, an expression of gratitude for their help?

She looked down at the Squid spaceship and felt overwhelmed. It was like connecting with an ancient secret buried in mankind's past. This vessel had been hidden underneath the stones for thousands of years, undetected by scientists' radar surveys of the site. It had waited beneath the ancient stones for exactly this moment.

Perhaps, she thought with a jolt, it had waited for her.

Just then the clouds parted and the ship shimmered in the sunlight, as if excited about being exhumed from its burial site. Its hull was a curious shade of blue, somewhere between turquoise and cerulean, and there was an airlock set in its side. The Arcturians had clearly noticed the doorway too because they had built a gangway over the excavation pit to reach it.

Just then, Casey felt something on the very edge of her consciousness. It was a sensation so faint she almost didn't notice it at first. Like a song being played at a super low volume. She gasped, surprised by its quiet intensity. It grew increasingly stronger as the sun's rays hit the ship, as if it was trying to get her attention.

"What's wrong?" Cheeze asked over his shoulder.

"It's the ship. I think it's calling to me."

"Well, that's perfectly normal and not freaky at all, is it?" he said with a nervous laugh. "What does it mean?"

"It means I have to get on board…"

24

BRING ME SCARLETT JOHANSSON!

The Reapers abandoned their van in a patch of woodland, deciding that the Goliaths guarding the edge of the dig site were less likely to spot them if they were on foot. Pete thought the Arcturians wouldn't be expecting an attack, especially not now that the Resistance's network had been broken up. His fear of Scratch gave him pause, though. She would know that Casey and the Reapers were still at large. She would also know that Pete had betrayed her. He could only imagine how furious she was.

While Pete fretted, the other boys unloaded a heavy Arcturian crate from the back of the van. It was purple and black, just like the ones in *SkyWake*.

"What is that?" he asked, intrigued.

"Rocket launchers," Fish grinned. "Commander Deacon's supply depot was like an Aladdin's cave." He cracked open the crate to reveal three long, cylindrical weapons familiar from the game. Players called them Jackhammers because, as their name suggested, they packed a punch.

"Oh, wow!" Pete murmured, shocked.

Fish's face fell.

"You don't think this was the kind of distraction your sister had in mind?"

Pete paused a moment. "I guess the more explosive our attack is, the better Casey's chances of getting onto the ship are," he decided.

"Explosive is right, bruv!" Elite said, clapping him on the shoulder. "We're gonna blow the Red Eyes all the way back to Arcturia." He did a little beatbox then launched into a rap: *"Yo, yo, my name's Elite, I'm the best sniper at a thousand feet. I've come to Stonehenge to stop the invasion. When the rockets go boom, I'll bring jubilation."* He struck a pose to finish.

Pete smiled. The boy's bravado was infectious – and very welcome given how many doubts Pete had about their hastily conceived plan. The Reapers had thrashed it out in broad strokes as they approached the site. The boys were going to create a distraction, attacking the site head on, while Cheeze kept the Goliaths busy. Casey would sneak on board the ship while everyone was busy.

The one wildcard was Haruto. He was the only remaining member of the Resistance they hadn't accounted for. Pete hoped the Resistance leader was far away in London.

There was a roar above them and an Arcturian shuttle flew over their heads. It was an elegant vessel with sculpted wings, a crimson body and a painted white stripe that ran across its hull from nose to tail. It came in low over Stonehenge, its engines burning as it set down on a landing pad on the far side of the site. Pete recognized the markings.

"The emperor's here," he told the Reapers. "The Arcturians must be ready to fire up the array."

"You think they've cracked the security code for it?" Elite asked.

"Triple points on *Blocka*, remember?" Brain said. "They must be close."

The group jogged across the muddy field that lay between the woods and the dig site. Brain, Elite and Fish carried a Jackhammer each. Although the rocket launchers were serious stuff, the boys were hardly a crack commando outfit. Pete thought of all the *SkyWake* games he'd ever played. The dig site felt like it could be part of the game, an unseen mission that no one had ever played before: sneak into the enemy base; avoid the giant Goliaths guarding the perimeter;

get to the objective. Perhaps it was the final stage; the boss battle. He was just glad that this time, whatever happened, he was on the right side.

On the edge of the dig site lay a cluster of portacabins laid out in neat rows. Some of the cabins were stacked two or three high, joined by metal staircases for access. The thicket of buildings gave the Reapers good cover from the Goliaths. As they crept between them, staying low, they spotted a group of thirty labourers being escorted from their bunk room by a squad of Red Eyes.

"Hold up," Brain hissed, ducking into cover behind a generator to avoid being spotted. The rest of the boys crowded low beside him. The labourers were fitted with shock shackles around their necks to stop them from escaping.

"Hey," Elite whispered, watching the labourers. "That's Jude!" He pointed to a petite girl. She looked totally defeated, her sparky defiance completely quashed.

"Do you think Marguerite and Babatunde are here too?" Fish asked. "We have to find her. I mean *them*."

"We don't have time for a rescue attempt," Pete warned, on edge. He wished he was as brave as the Reapers. Nothing seemed to faze them.

Fish bristled, annoyed. "They're our friends."

"Pete's right," Brain said, stepping in. "We have to stop the Arcturians first. After we do that, we can free everyone else."

"How are we gonna do this?" Elite asked, eager to get moving.

"I vote we do a hit and run," Brain said, patting his rocket launcher. "If we split up and attack from a bunch of different points, the Red Eyes will be confused about where we're coming from and how many of us there are. Once we've got their attention, we can pull back to the woods. Hopefully that will buy Casey enough time to get onto the ship."

"Tactics, bruv." Elite nodded. "I like it."

"What do you reckon, Pete?" Brain asked. "Will the Goliaths come after us?"

It took Pete a second to realize he was being asked his opinion.

"I reckon so." He nodded. It felt good to be included. "They'll be furious that the Resistance isn't dead and buried. They'll likely throw everything at us."

"Excellent. That's exactly what we want."

Fish looked back at the woods where they'd left the van.

"I'm not sure, you guys," he complained, rubbing his chin. "That's a long way to run across open ground. I mean, I can run fast, but not that fast. If those tripod things decide to come after us, we'll be dead before you can say War of the Worlds."

"Just imagine you're Tom Cruise, bruv," Elite suggested. "He runs like a whippet."

"I wonder where Tom Cruise is right now," Fish replied. "Him, The Rock, Chris Pine, Scarlett Johansson… Where are these guys when the world needs them?"

"You realize they're actors, right?" Brain asked. "They're not action heroes in real life."

"They're more like action heroes than we are. Have you ever fired a rocket launcher before? I bet Tom Cruise has. So why aren't they here?"

"I guess they're useless just like all the other adults," Elite decided. "They're probably all hiding in those billionaire apocalypse bunkers in New Zealand or something."

Fish harrumphed. "Scarlett Johansson, you broke my heart."

"We should probably get some height," Pete said, trying to get them back to discussing tactics. He looked at Brain. "If we climbed onto the roof of the portacabins we could get a decent vantage point to fire the Jackhammers from."

"Elevation!" Elite said and fist-bumped him. "Good call. First rule of sniping is controlling the high ground.

We'll make a Ghost Reaper out of you yet, Pete."

Pete smiled. He thought back to the shopping centre when he'd felt like a fifth wheel around these guys. How long ago that was! And how much had happened to him since then. Being here now, with the Reapers, made him feel like he belonged. He'd never felt like that hanging out with Xander.

"It's a plan, then," Brain agreed. "Me and Fish will take up position here. You guys circle the perimeter and attack from the other side. We'll try and catch them in a crossfire."

It took Pete and Elite fifteen minutes to sneak around the outer edge of the site. They moved without talking, using hand signals as they slid in and out of cover. It helped that the Red Eyes' attention was focussed on the stage that had been erected in front of the Squid spaceship. TV crews were positioned around it, their cameras ready to broadcast the activation of the array around the world. Pete knew the media angle inside out. This broadcast had been Xander's baby. If things had turned out differently, Xander would have been arriving onstage right about now.

Instead, a very different figure walked out under the bright lights. The emperor's long red robes flapped behind him as he stepped to the podium at the front of the stage, flanked by his white-clad imperial guard.

He carried his helmet under one arm and his free claw stroked the ruff around his neck, as if drawing the cameras' attention to it. He spoke in clipped English, his accent discordant and jarring.

"Citizens of Earth and Arcturia," he began, staring out into the cameras with his glassy black eyes. The stage lights glittered off his scales, producing dazzling rainbows of light. The emperor was formidable and threatening, but he lacked Xander's easy charm. Pete imagined everyone in front of their TVs at home. How many children – and perhaps even their parents – would be watching from behind the sofa in fear?

"Over the last four of your human years, Earth and Arcturia have worked together to achieve an impossible dream," the alien continued. "Piece by piece we have located the missing parts of an ancient alien artefact known as a psionic array. Built by a long-lost race, this artefact has the power to control whole galaxies. With it, Arcturia will bring order to the universe."

The emperor paused, as if expecting applause. Since there was no audience at the dig site he stood in silence a moment. Pete guessed it would be overlaid onto the broadcast to convince people watching at home that this was a moment to celebrate. He had seen enough of Xander's tricks to know how slick the production would look.

He wondered how close the Arcturian hackers were to actually cracking the access codes for the array. If the emperor was giving his victory speech, they must be on the cusp of unlocking the ancient vessel's secrets and activating it. He hoped Casey would hurry.

Movement caught his attention. He shielded his eyes from the rising sun and watched as a lone figure climbed up a telecommunications tower that stood opposite the stage. The tower was a tall metal lattice, set on a base of four steel feet. It tapered to a point several metres high like a baby version of the Eiffel Tower. It was covered with satellite dishes. Pete guessed they were being used to broadcast the speech across the globe. For a moment he assumed the figure was some kind of technician. As his eyes adjusted to the sun's glare, though, he realized it was actually a boy.

"Haruto!"

The Resistance leader was climbing swiftly up the tower, an Arcturian sniper rifle slung over his back. "What's he doing here?" Pete wondered aloud.

"I dunno, bruv," Elite replied. "But if I was gonna bet on it, I'd say he's planning to make the emperor's speech end with a bang."

Pete felt sick. "If he starts firing before Casey gets to the ship, we're stuffed!"

"Not a lot we can do, bruv."

"Yes, there is. Wait here!"

With that, Pete darted away on his own, leaving Elite to pull himself up onto the portacabins with the Jackhammer. Across the way, Brain and Fish were doing the same, getting ready to target the Goliaths that stood around the edge of the site.

Pete knew time was short. He sprinted between the portacabins, picking the fastest route that would get him to the telecommunications tower. At its base he found a thin metal ladder ran through the middle of the tower, stretching up to the platform at the very top. He hauled himself onto it and raced up the rungs, chasing after Haruto. As he climbed he had a panoramic view of the whole site. He could see the emperor onstage; the Reapers prepping their rocket launchers; and Cheeze's Goliath moving in on the excavated Squid spaceship. It was like watching the build-up to a car crash – all these moving parts, all about to smash into one another.

The ladder creaked and groaned as Pete climbed. By the time he emerged onto the wire mesh platform at the top of the tower, Haruto knew he was coming and lay in wait. He was dressed in a Red Cap uniform, complete with body armour and a tac vest stuffed with weapons and tools – a shock baton, plasma pistol and handcuffs. As soon as Pete stuck his head through the hatch, Haruto hauled him out and shoved the plasma pistol in his face.

"You!" he hissed, recognizing Pete from his television appearances.

"Don't shoot!" Pete begged, seeing the fury in the boy's face. "I'm on your side. I'm with the Resistance!"

He knew Haruto wouldn't recognize him as the informant on the motorcycle, as he'd made sure never to reveal his identity when they met up. The only thing Haruto knew about him was what he'd seen on TV. Pete with Xander and Scratch, doing the Arcturians' dirty work. No wonder the barrel of the boy's plasma pistol was rammed hard under his chin.

"The Resistance are gone," Haruto spat. "Your Red Eye friends rounded them all up." His finger inched around the pistol's trigger. "I ought to blow your head off for what you've done."

"Please…" Pete begged, struggling to get his words out. "The Reapers are here with Casey. My sister's trying to get onto the Squid ship."

Haruto recoiled in surprise. "Casey's your sister?"

"Yes, and she's our best chance of stopping the Red Eyes," Pete insisted. "I know you don't trust me. But trust her and her teammates."

Haruto's eyes blazed with fury. He grabbed Pete's arm and, in a swift movement, pulled the handcuffs off his tac vest. Before Pete could fight back, he was locked onto the railing at the top of the ladder.

"Stay here."

Pete felt his body sag. He'd managed to convince Haruto not to kill him, but not much else. He watched in defeat as Haruto prepped his Arcturian sniper rifle. He pulled out the barrel's tripod mount, before lying flat on his belly on the deck of the telecoms tower. He clamped his eye to the gun's high-tech scope, lining up the emperor in his sights.

"If you shoot, you'll ruin everything!" Pete warned. "The only way we can win is if Casey gets onto the ship."

"That lizard killed my parents!" Haruto yelled. "I'll never get another chance to take him down."

Pete looked across the site and caught sight of the Goliath piloted by Cheeze. It was almost at the spaceship. He guessed Casey was going to find some way to drop onto it and get inside. They were so close! But if Haruto started firing, the whole site would be shut down in minutes and his sister would never get on board.

"Please listen to me!" he begged. "What's the point of avenging your parents if the Red Eyes still win?"

"Why on Earth would I listen to you? You're a collaborator."

"You've been listening to me for months! I'm the

person who told you where to find the food convoys and the arms depots. I'm the one who met you in the shadows. I'm the one who fed you information about the Red Eyes' troop movements. It was me on the motorbike, all those times."

"You're the informer?" Haruto asked in disbelief. "Why would *you* help us?"

"Because I thought the Resistance could stop the Red Eyes!" Pete exclaimed. "I thought you guys were going to save the day. But you couldn't save yourselves, let alone the planet! Don't you get it? We need Casey. She's the only one who can finish this."

"You're a liar!"

Pete could see he was never going to get through to him. Haruto was too stubborn, too angry. He tugged against his handcuffs hopelessly. Haruto ignored him and lined up his shot through the scope. Pete strained to see the Reapers on the ground below. He wished he had some way to warn them that his plan had gone wrong.

There was a hum as the sniper rifle drew power from its battery packs.

"Please don't do this," Pete whispered.

A searing burst of energy tore from the rifle's barrel. The bolt of plasma flew right towards the emperor's head, cleaving it in two.

"No!"

It took Pete a second to realize something was wrong. Down on the stage the emperor didn't scream or fall. His split-apart head simply flickered and glitched. Then it became whole again as if nothing had happened.

"What the—" Haruto exclaimed, tearing his eye from the scope to look. "It's a hologram!"

He was right. The emperor wasn't standing on the stage at all. He was somewhere else, safe and secure, projecting his image. Pete glanced over at his shuttle on the landing pad across the site, guessing he was on there.

"They must have known I was coming!" Haruto raged. He looked at Pete as if it was all his fault. The boy didn't know what to say. Had Scratch guessed their plan? Or perhaps she had followed Haruto from the weapons depot? Either way the attack had failed before it had even started.

There was a flurry of movement on the ground as the Red Eyes launched into action. Troops ran in all directions, ready to secure the alien ship. The three Goliaths on the perimeter of the site jerked into action, alerted to the news that the site had been infiltrated. Pete imagined everyone at home watching this unfold on TV. Xander would approve. This was a guaranteed ratings winner.

"Uncuff me," he begged Haruto. "We've got to get out of here."

The Resistance leader stared at him, paralysed with shock. A dozen drones were already flying towards the tower, looking for the would-be assassin who'd dared to try and assassinate the Arcturian leader. Pete guessed that the next dig site he and Haruto would see would be their graves.

"Please … Haruto!"

Saying the boy's name made him jolt back to life. He bent down next to Pete and unlocked the cuffs. The telecoms tower started to shake as a Goliath stepped towards them. It swivelled its guns, locking on. The blood drained from Haruto's face. His sniper rifle would be about as much use as a nerf gun against this giant machine. Pete struggled to free himself from the handcuffs. The Goliath's guns throbbed and glowed. It took another step and—

WHOMPF! A rocket flew across the dig site and exploded against the machine's body. Its legs flexed with the force of the impact, bending on their segmented joints and releasing a banshee wail. A thin trail of smoke led to the portacabin where Elite was crouched on the roof. He was frantically trying to reload. The Goliath, furious at his sneak attack, spun around to face him. Forgetting all about Pete and Haruto, it opened fire and strafed the portacabins with a furious burst of plasma. Elite jumped off the rooftop just in time.

"Haruto!" Pete yelled. "We've got to move!" He hauled the Resistance leader towards the ladder. A drone buzzed around them as they descended, its fisheye lens beaming their image to the Red Eyes around the site. Pete hurried his pace and whispered a silent prayer, hoping that Casey would make it to the spaceship in time.

25

EJECT!

The control console in the hijacked Goliath screamed a dozen alarms in a variety of different pitches. Casey imagined all of them translated roughly as: *You're gonna die!* In a heartbeat, they'd gone from walking-into-the-heart-of-the-enemy-camp-in-perfect-disguise, to having a giant target painted on their back that said: *Shoot me!*

The moment Haruto opened fire at the emperor, the Goliaths at the dig site had communicated with one another. When Cheeze didn't give them the right response, they realized that there was an imposter among them. Two of them locked onto Cheeze's Goliath, while the third broke off to attack Haruto and Pete at the telecommunications tower.

Casey held on tight as the Goliath was hit by plasma fire from the enemy vehicles. The machine's legs buckled so badly that, for a terrifying moment, she thought they were going down. Cheeze, hunched over the controls, managed to right it. He seemed to have found his rhythm and was now in sync with the three-legged vehicle. Years of video gaming was serving him well.

"Can you still get me to the spaceship?" Casey asked, looking out at the excavated Squid vessel. As she did, she saw the streak of a rocket and realized that the rest of the Reapers had begun their attack down on the ground. She had to make the most of their distraction.

Cheeze twisted the Goliath around, trying to avoid a blast of plasma fire.

"I'm taking heavy damage," he warned. "I'm not going to be able to set you down on the ground."

"How do I get out?"

"There's a hatch in the floor."

Casey ran over to the hatch and pressed the buttons to unlock it. There was a hiss as it opened. Her stomach heaved as she saw how high up they were. The landscape below the Goliath pitched and rolled as it defended itself from attack. Cheeze hit a button and a steel cable, like the one that had whipped at her on the roof of the car park, dropped from the Goliath's body to form a makeshift escape rope.

"How will you get out?" Casey asked. It wouldn't be long before the Goliath's shields were down and the three-legged machine was torn to pieces. She knew Cheeze wouldn't be able to abseil down the line.

"The cockpit's got an ejector seat," her friend reassured her. "It's a one-way ticket for a wild ride."

Casey stared through the hatch at the ground below. It was such a long drop. She remembered the sensation of standing on the top of the highest diving board at her local swimming pool. You stood on the edge and stared at the water, trying to trick your brain into making the leap. This was the same. Except there wasn't any water to break her fall. She pulled on a pair of padded pilot's gloves she'd found in the storage rack beside the hatch, hoping they'd stop her from shredding her hands on the cable.

"If you're gonna go, go now!" Cheeze yelled.

Casey paused, wracked by indecision. She looked back at Cheeze one last time. She didn't want to leave him. Not like this.

"Go!" he shouted as another explosion rocked the Goliath. The interior lights dimmed and crackled, the power surging through the vehicle as it diverted everything it had to its shields.

Casey grabbed onto the cable, linking her feet around it. The gloves took the friction as she slid down its length. The air was thick with the bitter smell of burning plasma. She hit the ground too fast and was flung onto the grass. She rolled onto her back and saw the enormous Goliath pass over her head.

Pulling herself up, she hurried across the excavation site. Her eyes were on the gangway that led across the pit to the airlock in the Squid ship. The closer she got, the more she could feel the ship calling to her. It sounded like a distress beacon – an insistent, looping telepathic call searching for someone who would respond and help it. Had this ship been abandoned when the Squids departed from Earth? Or had it been left as a secret, a gift waiting to be discovered? Or perhaps it was an invitation? A means by which humans could head into space and reconnect with the ancient race that had helped them millennia before? The more the ship sang to her, the more she wondered if it was looking for a crew. Maybe it needed someone to activate it after all these years buried beneath the earth. But she also remembered the Sirens in Greek mythology, who sang to sailors to lure them to their doom. She prayed she wasn't walking into a trap.

Another explosion rocked the battlefield, shaking her back to her senses. The enemy Goliaths had closed in on Cheeze's position and were attacking him in a pincer movement. He was fighting valiantly, the body of his huge machine spinning left and right on its central axis as he tried to defend himself against their incoming fire. It was obvious he couldn't hold out much longer, though. She just hoped he could rescue his hoverchair before he was forced to eject.

She ducked behind an Arcturian digging machine as a squad of Red Eyes ran past, hurrying to the portacabins the Reapers were firing their Jackhammers from. As soon as they'd gone, Casey snuck forward until she could see the Squid vessel dead ahead. It was huge and mysterious, its hull glittering as the morning sun's rays made contact with its surface. The alien alloy seemed even stranger close up, the metal swirling and clouding as if it was alive.

She sprinted for the narrow gangway that was suspended over the pit. Before she could reach it, a tall figure stepped out from behind a stack of supply crates and blocked her way.

"I knew you'd come," Scratch hissed, her obsidian eyes glinting with hatred. Her energy sword burst into life in her hand. Its blade hummed hungrily.

Casey backed up, her heart sinking. She was unarmed and alone.

"I don't want to fight you," she said quietly.

The words were barely out of her mouth before Scratch made a lunge for her, the energy sword whirling over her head with savage ferocity. Casey ducked and the sword tip hit the grass, burning through the soil. Scratch pulled it free and swung again, forcing Casey to retreat in a wide circle until her feet stumbled onto the gangway. She found herself on the narrow platform that led across the excavation pit to the spaceship. She backed up along it, trapped. Scratch followed her, sensing she had the advantage.

"I have waited a long time for this," the alien said. Her salmon-pink tongue slithered between her lips, darting left and right in anticipation. With a jolt, Casey realized this was the inevitable showdown. They had been heading towards this ever since their very first tussle in Starbucks in the shopping centre.

She looked around, desperate to find a weapon. She cursed herself for not being better prepared. She'd exhausted herself fighting the Goliath in the car park and now she had nothing left to give.

No guns.

No sword.

No flow.

"Please," Casey stammered, backing along the gangway towards the airlock on the spaceship. "We don't have to be enemies." She could hear the desperation in her voice, and she knew Scratch would be repulsed by it. The Arcturians hated cowardice.

"Only someone without a weapon would say that," the overseer hissed. "You are weak, *Cay-See*. Weak and helpless. I am going to finish you. And when I am done,

I am going to gut that traitorous little brother of yours, too. How much better the world will be without you both in it."

Casey realized it wasn't just her life at stake here. It was everything and everyone she cared about, too. There was no way to avoid this final battle, no matter how much she wanted to. She couldn't get out of it any more than one of the characters in *Street Fighter II* could get out of their endless bouts.

Thinking about *Street Fighter II* gave her an idea.

She stared at her empty hands.

Maybe she wasn't unarmed after all.

In that moment, Scratch attacked again. She held her sword two-handed and brought it high above her head, ready to strike. Casey saw it coming, but dodged a second too late. The energy sword slashed into her forearm. She screamed as it burned through her flesh.

"You've nowhere left to go," Scratch mocked. "Unless you want to jump again?" She nodded to the pit below them. Casey remembered their gladiatorial fight on the space station above Hosin and how she had leaped off the stage into the void beneath it to escape. She wasn't sure she could pull that trick off twice.

Sensing that she was finished, Scratch let out a screeching war cry and then rushed along the gangway. Her cowl flapped behind her, and her sword twirled above her head. She was ready to deliver the finishing blow.

Casey froze, preparing herself for the sword's impact.

Time seemed to slow down and, as it did, she felt her hands tingling. They crackled with a blue, electrical heat that made the hairs on her arms stand to attention. She shaped the energy in her hands, forming it into a perfect sphere. She hadn't tried to summon the power. It had just appeared when she needed it most.

Scratch continued her berserker charge along the gangway, convinced that victory was almost hers. Casey cupped the energy ball between her palms. She held it a moment, transfixed by its swirling beauty. Then she hurled it towards her Arcturian nemesis.

"Hadouken!"

The energy ball flew along the gangway. Scratch screamed and tried to block it with her sword. But the ball ripped through the energy blade and smacked into the alien's chest, knocking her backwards. Her sword clattered across the gangway and fell into the pit. Scratch followed right behind it. She plummeted over the railings with a terrified, inhuman screech.

Exhausted by the effort, Casey collapsed onto the gangway. She felt weaker than ever. Each time she used these abilities, they seemed to take an even greater toll on her. As she lay there, catching her breath, a scaly claw appeared over the lip of the gangway.

"*Cay-See!*" Scratch hissed. "Help me!"

Casey crawled over. Scratch was dangling over the pit, hanging onto the edge of the gangway with a gnarled claw. Panic flared in her eyes. "Please!" the alien begged.

"Take my hand," Casey said and reached through the railings to her. Scratch swung herself up and grabbed the girl's forearm with her free claw.

Casey grunted as she took Scratch's weight. It felt like her shoulder might dislocate. Her other arm, injured by the energy blade's slash, was next to useless. "I can't hold you," she groaned.

"I know," Scratch hissed, her mouth contorting into a vicious smile. Then, without warning, she released her grip on the gangway. Casey screamed as she was pulled forward by Scratch's weight into the railings and crushed against them. She couldn't move. She couldn't breathe.

I am going to die here.

She would have done, too, if Pete hadn't arrived.

Her brother came sprinting along the gangway, rocking it with his weight. Seeing what was happening, he grabbed Casey first, trying to pull her away from the bars. When that didn't work, he lashed out at Scratch's claw with his foot, stomping on it in a blind, desperate rage. The alien hissed at him and squeezed her talons deeper into Casey's arm. Frantic, Pete dropped to his knees at the edge of the gangway. He bent low and sank his teeth into Scratch's hand as hard as he could, drawing blood. He ignored the sickening taste of her scales.

Scratch screeched in agony. She let go of Casey and fell into the pit, plummeting like a stone. There was a sickening crunch as her body hit the side of the Squid spaceship below and then landed in the mud at the very bottom of the excavations.

Pete looked down at her as she lay in the dirt, her cowl covered in mud. She didn't move. He waited a moment, just to be sure.

"Thank you," Casey whispered on the gangway beside him. The anger that she'd felt towards her little brother for so long now seemed a distant memory. He had come back for her. He cared about her. Of course he did!

She tried to stand, to get to the Squid spaceship. But her legs wouldn't listen. They refused to lift her. She was too weak.

The gangway vibrated beneath her as more people came running along it.

"Guys!" she heard Pete shout. "Help me!"

Brain and Elite were suddenly beside her.

"Lift her up," Brain instructed. Several pair of hands grabbed her, hauling her onto her feet and supporting her weight. She saw Cheeze and Fish there, too. Then Haruto came sprinting down the gangway. He turned and fired at a squad of Red Eyes. The sound of plasma fire jolted Casey to her senses. Every Red Eye at the dig site was coming after them.

"I can stand," she said, regaining her footing.

"Everyone get inside the ship," Brain ordered the group. "Cheeze, Haruto, cover us."

They ran down the gangway towards the airlock. As they approached Casey felt the ship reaching out to her more strongly than ever. The airlock door swished open. It was as if it had been waiting for exactly this moment to unlock itself. As soon as they were all inside it shut behind them, locking the pursuing Red Eyes outside. Clearly the ship didn't want anyone but Casey and her friends inside.

No one was sure how they should feel about that.

26

DOES ANYONE KNOW HOW TO FLY THIS THING?

The interior of the Squid spaceship was cold and spacious. The walls glistened with a frozen blue light that made it look as if the vessel had been carved from an ice block. They could hear plasma fire outside, but the hull's protective thickness made it seem distant and unimportant.

"How long will it hold them for?" Fish asked, eyeing the door as a blast of plasma scorched it.

"No idea, but they won't want to damage the ship if they can help it," Brain said. "This is the key to everything they want."

"Should we sabotage it, then?" Haruto asked, scanning the interior for some weakness in the ship's design that he could exploit.

"Casey's got a plan," Brain told him testily. "Just take a breath."

"She can barely stand," Haruto retorted, looking at her with a mixture of pity and annoyance.

"She's got this, bruv," Elite said. "Back off."

Casey heard the argument play out, although she struggled to follow it. The ship continued to call her, its insistent silent signal buzzing in her brain. It seemed to be guiding her.

"This way," she croaked. "Up this ramp."

Elite and Brain helped her up a smooth ramp that stretched into darkness. There were no steps anywhere to be seen. The whole vessel was designed for Squid tentacles rather than human feet.

"At least they've made it accessible," Cheeze muttered wryly as his hoverchair ascended the ramp.

"Hey, are you guys feeling that?" Brain asked, uncertainty spreading across his face.

"Like a tingling?" said Fish.

"More like a ringing," Elite said. "In my head."

"It's the ship," Pete whispered. "It knows we're here."

"That's ridiculous," Haruto scoffed. "I don't hear anything."

"This leads to the flight deck," Casey murmured as they neared the top of the ramp. In her mind's eye she saw an image of three ancient Squids, the crew, slithering up this very ramp millennia ago.

"How do you know that?" Fish asked. He noticed

the distant expression on her face and scowled. "Is she OK?" he asked Cheeze.

"She's OK," his friend replied.

"You're sure? Because she doesn't look OK to me."

Cheeze glanced from Casey to Fish and then back to Casey again. "No, I'm not sure. Not really," he admitted.

"OK, then. Glad we cleared that up. Good to get clarity."

"I'm fine," Casey croaked. She pulled herself free from Brain and Elite's hands and stumbled onto the flight deck. She stood in the middle of it, as if in a trance. A control console lit up as she approached. It was smooth and blank and made from the same, blue-tinted material as the rest of the ship. There were no buttons or switches, just an oval indentation shaped like the paddles at the end of the Squids' tentacles. Instinctively, Casey reached her hand towards it.

She jolted as the connection was made, the force of it jerking her body. A flicker of light appeared in the middle of the deck and took the shape of a Squid. Its enormous, bulbous body was rendered as an incredibly realistic 3D hologram.

"Xolotl!" Fish cried, recognizing her. The Squid's tentacles undulated in greeting, and she slithered towards them.

Haruto gasped and raised his sniper rifle. He was

the only one who'd never seen a Bactu before and he assumed the alien was about to attack them. Elite snatched the weapon from his hands.

"She's a friend. Be cool."

"We knew we were right to put our faith in you," Xolotl said, her silent voice appearing inside all their heads at once. "Thank you." She reached out a tentacle and caressed Casey's cheek. The hologram's light flickered against her skin. Casey, lost in her trance, didn't respond.

"Tell us what to do," Brain urged the alien. "Casey's weak and the Red Eyes are right outside. We're running out of time."

Xolotl turned to the boy. "When Casey activates the array, the pieces that the Red Eyes have dug up across the Earth will link. Together they will amplify her telepathic power."

"Amplify it how?" Brain asked, eager to understand.

"By turning it into a single burst of energy. The Bactu left the array on Earth in the hope humans would one day find and activate it. It is designed as an intergalactic beacon, a means of communicating with other caretaker races."

"I thought it was a weapon," Haruto muttered.

"It could be," Xolotl told him. "It's powerful enough to amplify Casey's flow. A blast of Confusion could incapacitate every Arcturian in the galaxy permanently. How you use it is your choice. Whatever you decide, though, it can only be used once."

A sudden explosion shook the ship, making Xolotl's hologram glitch and flicker in mid-air. The Red Eyes were pounding the hull with more than just plasma rifles now, perhaps realizing that they were close to losing control of the vessel for ever.

The boys looked at one another, anxious.

"You can't leave a decision like that to us," Cheeze cried, looking at Casey's trembling body as she stood at the control panel. "We're just kids. We can't decide for the entire planet."

Xolotl turned to face him. "Millennia ago, the Bactu came to Earth as caretakers," she explained. "We met humanity when you were just children, still uncertain of your purpose. We encouraged you to grow and to develop. Yet we never told you what to do. We didn't force you to obey like the Arcturians do to those they enslave. We didn't ask you to follow us, or pledge allegiance to us. Yes, humanity has made mistakes. But mistakes are how we learn."

Pete stared at the ground, feeling the weight of the Squid's words. They felt somehow personal.

"Enough of this cryptic mumbo-jumbo!" Fish yelled, out of patience. "Just tell us what to do!"

Xolotl gave no sign she had heard him. "Whatever you decide here," the alien continued, "there is no wrong decision. It is your time now. Are you ready?"

Before anyone could answer, Casey groaned and slumped over the console. Pete and Brain caught her before she hit the floor. Seeing what was happening, Cheeze spun around in his hoverchair to face the alien.

"You can't do this to her!" he shouted. "She's too weak. She can't do it on her own!"

Xolotl's tentacles rippled as if amused by it all. "She's not alone," she told him. "She has you. All of you. What you need to do is—"

There was another thud and the ship shook from bow to stern. The hologram flickered, then glitched and vanished.

"Xolotl!" Cheeze shouted. "Come back! All we need to do is *what*?"

"Well, that's just brilliant," Fish said.

The Reapers looked at one another, uncertain what to do next. Casey opened her eyes, coming to. She groaned in pain.

"I have no idea who that octopus thing was or what they were talking about," Haruto said, gesturing to the empty air where Xolotl had been a moment ago, "but we've got to stop the Red Eyes. If this ship is a weapon, we either need to use it to destroy them, or we destroy it before they can get hold of it."

"Yo, Squids aren't about destroying people," Elite said, shaking his head. "They believe in looking after them."

"Stopping the Red Eyes is looking after everyone," Pete said. "The Arcturians don't respect anything except violence and power. The whole reason they've been searching for the array is to use it as a weapon against every other race in the universe."

"What do you think, Casey?" Cheeze asked, turning around in his hoverchair. Everyone held their breath, waiting for her response. She, after all, was the only one who could make this happen ... whatever the decision.

"I can't do it," Casey said, struggling to form her words. "Whatever it is I'm supposed to do. I'm not strong enough."

Somewhere on the other side of the ship there was a clanging thud and then a high-pitched screech. It sounded like the Arcturians were cutting their way through the hull.

"C'mon!" Haruto shouted, pulling Casey back towards the control panel. "If we don't destroy them, they'll destroy us!"

"That's not a reason to attack them!" Brain cried. "We have a choice."

"Damn the choice!" Haruto pushed Casey the last

few steps towards the console.

"I can't," she moaned. "I just can't."

"You have to!" Haruto yelled, shaking her in a rage. He was desperate to take his revenge on the Arcturians.

"Hey!" Pete shouted, pushing Haruto away from Casey. "Leave my sister alone."

"Don't fight…" Casey murmured weakly. "We're supposed to be on the same side."

"Yeah," Fish said. "We're a team, right? Ghost Reapers for the win! And," he added hurriedly, indicating Pete and Haruto, "all the rest of us too."

"Of course!" Brain cried, his face lighting up with excitement. "That's it! It's about all of us!"

"What are you on about, bruv?" Elite demanded.

"The Squids said this flow power was in all humans," Brain explained.

"You mean it's not just Casey who's special?" Cheeze asked, picking up the thread of thought.

Pete gasped. "That's why we're feeling the ship too. It's reaching out to everyone."

"Quickly," Cheeze ordered. "Get around the console."

The Reapers and Pete moved into a circle around the strange console in the centre of the room. Only Haruto stood apart, unable or unwilling to understand what they were trying to do. Casey reached out a hand to the control panel. It glowed blue in anticipation of her touch. She tensed, feeling its charge again.

"How do we do this?" Elite asked, looking around at the others.

"What would the Squids do if they were here?" Cheeze asked.

"Get inside our heads?" Fish suggested, remembering how the Squids communicated telepathically.

"Don't you remember?" Brain asked. "In the cave on Hosin they lay in the dark, their tentacles touching. That was how they created the mindscape. It was like a network. No one in charge, everyone equal. They took their power from one another. That's what we need to do too."

He held out his hand to Elite.

"Seriously, bruv? We're gonna hold hands?"

"Just trust me."

Elite sighed and took his hand. "Your palm's all sweaty."

Cheeze did the same. Then Fish.

"Is this like a seance or something?" he complained.

"Just get in here," Brain ordered, grabbing him.

"Wait," Cheeze said. "It should be all of us." He looked over at Pete and Haruto. "Come on."

Pete hesitated, but Casey beckoned to him. She squeezed his hand with what little strength she had left.

Pete held out his free hand to Haruto, who stared back at them all, shaking his head.

"No way."

"Please," Pete begged. "This is how we win."

Haruto grunted. For a moment Casey thought he was going to turn and stalk away. Instead, he paused and looked around the ship. His eyes narrowed as he stared into the gloomy recesses that surrounded them. He looked puzzled.

Pete smiled. "You can hear it, can't you? The ship? It's calling to you, too."

Haruto didn't reply. He just stepped into the circle and took Pete and Fish's hands in his. "Let's get on with it," he said.

Casey stood a little taller, drawing strength from her friends. She took a deep breath and felt her mind emptying, the stress and worry slowly silenced as her thoughts focussed solely on the job at hand. She remembered the feeling of flow she'd first had playing *Space Invaders*. She remembered the sensation when Xolotl had reached into her mind and unlocked the door for her. Finally, she recalled the feeling she'd had when defeating Scratch.

This felt like all those moments distilled into one.

She was keenly aware of each boy. Their minds overlapped into hers in a mishmash of thoughts and emotions. More than anything, though, she felt a rushing wave of power that came from each of her friends. It rose through the circle they'd created with their hands, feeding through her and into the console in the centre of the spaceship.

The ship began to shake and shudder. Its lights pulsed a deeper blue. There was a groaning creak of metal and, for a moment, Casey thought the Red Eyes had successfully breached the hull. Then the ship ascended into the air, leaving the resting place it had patiently occupied for the last few millennia. The blast shields on the windows opened, flooding the flight deck with daylight. They saw the ancient standing stones topple over the bow of the ship, falling to the ground below. Casey gasped – sorry for the destruction of such an iconic landmark, yet aware they were making history.

The Squid spaceship hovered in the sky above Stonehenge, its systems powering up. Casey heard the other pieces of the array chirrup around the globe back to the vessel in a kind of call and response. She wondered what chaos was happening at the other dig sites from Central America to Egypt to the Pacific as the signal from the Squid vessel linked the beacons together.

She looked around the group, already knowing

what they wanted to do with the vast power now at their disposal.

"Go for it," Brain told her.

Casey willed the ship to send its message into the cosmos. There was a crackle and a shudder as the vessel drew power from all the beacons the Red Eyes had excavated across the planet. Then an enormous column of energy burst out of the ship and charged upwards into the atmosphere. An emergency call for assistance had been dispatched into the ether, broadcast across the depths of space to who knew where.

It was done.

"Is something supposed to happen?" Elite asked after a couple of seconds had passed. "We fired the array, right? So why is nothing happening?"

Outside the ship, the Red Eyes' forces were assembling. Two Goliaths strode towards the Squid vessel as it hung in mid-air, their guns blasting its hull. Dropships emerged from the clouds above them, bringing reinforcements. Even the Red Eye grunts on the ground were taking pot-shots at the vessel with their plasma rifles.

"They're going to blast us out of the sky!" Fish yelled. "Can't we escape? Hit the warp drive or whatever it is?"

"You think I know how to fly this thing?" Casey asked, incredulous.

A barrage of plasma fire rocked the vessel, knocking it off balance. The Reapers were thrown across the flight deck, their circle of hands broken as they lost their footing. The ship pitched and rolled.

"We're going down like the *Titanic*!" Fish cried.

An alarm blared and the ship's systems righted the vessel. Casey pulled herself back to her feet. As she did, she saw an incredible sight through the flight deck's enormous windows.

The sky above Stonehenge began to fill with the strangest-looking spaceships Casey had ever seen. They appeared out of thin air one by one, slamming into the Earth's atmosphere from hyperspace. One second they weren't there, the next they were. The ships were huge – bigger than anything Casey and her friends had seen during their adventures – and built in strange geometric designs that seemed impossible to the human eye.

"Who are they?" Brain asked, amazed by what he was seeing.

"I think they're the caretakers," Casey whispered.

On the ground below the Squid ship, the attacking Red Eyes stood in stunned silence and stared up into the sky. It took the commanders a few seconds to recover from their shock and issue the order to open fire at the new arrivals. As always the Arcturians were happy to respond to anything they didn't understand or like with violence.

The battle lasted less than ten seconds.

As soon as the Red Eyes fired, the caretaker ships retaliated. Their systems obliterated the Goliaths and the dropships with weapons of enormous magnitude and ferocity. The Arcturians were completely outgunned.

A lone vessel streaked low across the fields at full speed, escaping into the near distance before arcing upwards into the sky. It was the emperor's shuttle. With their commander-in-chief gone, the remaining Red Eyes laid down their weapons and did something that no Arcturian had ever done before... They surrendered.

In the aftermath of the battle, the caretaker ships hung in the sky, strange and mysterious. The Reapers held their breath, uncertain what would happen next. A trilling sound echoed around the flight deck and then the holographic display flashed with an incoming communication. An alien face appeared on-screen. It was covered in hair and its mouth had long, thin teeth like giant pins. Its large eyes, though, were gentle and inquisitive. It looked surprised, as if it had been expecting to see Squids not humans.

"Who triggered the ancient Bactu beacon?" the alien demanded. Its surprisingly melodic alien language was translated into English by the ship's systems.

"Are we in trouble?" Fish whispered. "Ask them if we're in trouble."

Casey stood up tall.

"We triggered it," she said. "Together."

The alien stared at them. Its large eyes blinked once, long and slow.

"Then you are the Bactu's successors. Welcome."

27

THE NEXT LEVEL

Everyone knew that things would never be the same again after the Red Eyes' defeat. The planet was in ruins, its major cities destroyed by the invasion and the last four years of occupation. What was worse, the world's politicians and business leaders had been exposed as liars and frauds. A reckoning was inevitable.

Casey and her friends retreated from the chaos, heading home to reunite with their families. They watched the aftermath of their adventure on the news like everyone else. They were hailed as heroes for stopping the invaders. But, over the next few months, the bigger questions remained unanswered. How should the world move on now that the Arcturians were vanquished? The Red Eyes' pursuit of power at all costs had forced the human race to take a long hard look at itself. Nobody liked what they saw.

In the meantime, word came that the Arcturian empire had collapsed. The caretakers, summoned by the array from distant parts of the universe, had freed planet after planet from the Red Eyes' grip until the invaders were forced to retreat to the safety of their home world, Arcturia. Seeing his domain destroyed in a matter of weeks, the emperor vanished from sight. There were rumours that Scratch, who had somehow survived her fall, was planning a coup to replace him.

As Earth debated its future, the enormous caretaker spaceships waited patiently in the sky. Unlike the Arcturian vessels they replaced, they were a benign presence. In the weeks after activating the array, Casey liked to get up early in the morning and sit in the garden staring up at them. The weather always seemed to part around them, the clouds splitting across their curved flanks, the sun glinting off their strange metal forms, creating glimmering points of light across their bows. Not even the rain seemed to touch them.

There was something reassuring about their presence and, even though their occupants were content not to interfere in Earth's affairs, she knew they were waiting to see what would happen. By firing up the array, humans had proved themselves worthy of attention from these ancient alien races. The only question that remained was whether or not humanity could get its act together and convince them to stay.

"How long do you think they'll wait?" Pete asked, joining her in the garden one morning. The February air was crisp and brittle, but the sky was blue. The first promise of spring was all around as snowdrops poked out of the dead leaves that scattered the flower beds and blackbirds pecked the frosty ground.

"Who knows?" Casey murmured, pulling her coat around her. "I guess they want to see if we can settle our differences. Grow into our new role. I hear there are elections next week to nominate a global council. Imagine it, a world government with every nation on Earth represented equally. No more war, no more hunger, no more bickering among ourselves. They say we're going to look outwards, to the stars, from now on."

"We really have grown up, haven't we?"

Casey was surprised by the maturity in her brother's voice. She wondered if she would ever get used to the way the age difference between them had been erased for ever.

"The caretakers want us to step up," she said. "When we're ready they're willing to share their tech with us and show us how to hone the psi-powers the Squids say we're capable of developing."

A blackbird hopped across the patio, oblivious to them.

"I'm worried we'll mess it all up," Pete confessed. "It's so much, so quickly. Humans can be really stupid sometimes."

"It's going to be OK," Casey told him. The certainty in her voice surprised her as well as Pete. "The Arcturians have done us a favour. If they hadn't invaded, we might never have learned what we're capable of. Both good and bad."

Pete sat with her a moment longer, staring up at the caretaker ship overhead. The size of it never ceased to amaze him.

"What are you thinking?" Casey asked.

"Just about Dad. You know I still have these?" He pulled out their father's army dog tags from under his shirt. The two silver metal tags glinted in the sun, attached on a chain around his neck.

"I gave them to you, before we set off for Hosin," Casey remembered. "I thought you'd lost them."

Pete pulled a face. "I never took them off. Not once in all these years." He ran them through his hands, letting his fingers play over the letters that spelled out their dad's name.

"He'd be proud of us, I think," Casey said quietly. "I mean, everything that's happened would totally fry his mind. But I think, if we explained it all to him, he'd say we did a good job…"

"I made a lot of mistakes," Pete whispered, not willing to meet her eyes.

"We both did. But we learned from them, right?" Casey patted his shoulder gently.

Pete took the chain that held the dog tags together and stretched it between his hands until it snapped.

"We should have one each," he said, handing her a metal tag.

Casey smiled, her eyes brimming with tears. "Dad would have liked that," she told him. "Thank you."

There was a shout from the back door.

"Casey! Pete! Your friends are calling you!" Mum cried, holding Casey's phone in her hand.

"We'll be there in a minute," Casey told her.

She stood up and stretched. She was looking forward to speaking to her friends. She was glad that even after the Reapers had returned home, they'd all stayed in touch. Fish had gone back to Glasgow to his dad and brothers. They'd reopened the chip shop as a community food hub to help feed people as the city got back on its feet. Marguerite had visited him for the opening ceremony. Casey had a sneaking suspicion the redheaded girl was going to remain on the scene for a while.

Elite was back at home in South London, reunited with his parents and his little sister. She was still having nightmares about the Red Eyes, as were so many other people, both young and old. He was performing raps about fighting the Red Eyes that he posted on YouTube. They were moderately popular.

Brain had begun his applied mathematics degree at Oxford University. He said maths would be more in demand now than ever, given that humanity was reaching for the stars. Haruto, Jude and Babatunde were delivering motivational talks about their resistance efforts to audiences around the world. The story of how they'd continued to fight back against impossible odds had won them many fans.

Cheeze was the only one who hadn't returned home. He'd earned the attention of the government's top scientists who wanted to pick his brains about the hoverchair he'd assembled and about all the Arcturian tech he'd seen during their adventures. He was staying in London permanently, accompanied by his parents, which suited Casey just fine. She enjoyed his company most of all.

Although the Reapers had been messaging one another constantly since the end of their adventure, today was the first time they'd all been online together since Stonehenge. No one was quite sure if they could go back to how things were before, playing games together as a team. Would it feel weird after having been through so much in real life? Casey hoped it wouldn't. She missed the familiar rhythm of playing and chatting and doing things together in the virtual world ... things that wouldn't get you fried or zapped or abducted or killed in real life if they went wrong. She was looking forward, she realized, to some escapism.

"What do you think we should play?" Pete asked as they crossed the garden. He was chuffed to be invited into the Ghost Reapers as their newest member. Casey had even promised him she'd get some new hoodies printed with the team's logo.

"I really don't mind," Casey laughed. "Just as long as it isn't *SkyWake*."

"Yeah," Pete agreed as they headed inside. "I think we've all had more than enough of that game."

Casey took one last look at the caretaker spaceship that hung patiently overhead. She smiled, safe in the knowledge that it would still be waiting for her when she returned.

Acknowledgements

This is the third and final book in the *SkyWake* series. I always knew the story would end back on Earth with Casey and her brother Pete reunited and the Red Eyes vanquished. But the twists and turns the story has taken along the way have surprised me as much as I hope they've surprised you, the reader.

Writing this series has been a thrill and a privilege. I'm lucky to have had an absolutely brilliant team at Walker Books in the UK and New Zealand/Australia supporting me. Huge thanks to my fantastic editor, Emma Lidbury; designer Anna Robinette; copyeditor Jenny Glencross; Kirsten Cozens in Publicity; James Fraser for his stunning cover; and everyone else who's worked so hard on this book. Thank you to my super-agent Ella Kahn and to my amazing team (Louise, Isobel and Alice) at home.

Finally, thank you to all the readers, librarians, teachers, booksellers and fellow authors who've championed the *SkyWake* series since it started. You all deserve a place on the high score table. Until next time, go with the flow!

"A rollercoaster of a read for gamers and sci-fi fans."
Kirsty Applebaum

"Brilliantly original."
Liz Hyder

Jamie Russell is a former contributing editor of *Total Film* magazine turned screenwriter and author. After writing about movies and video games for two decades, he made his fiction debut with *SkyWake Invasion* and its sequel, *SkyWake Battlefield*. He loves reading sci-fi novels and is a passionate gamer. His favourite video game is *Overwatch*, although he also plays lots of *Fortnite* and *Dark Souls* and has an occasional blast on retro classic *Space Invaders*. He lives in Shrewsbury in Shropshire with his family, a crazy rescue dog and a grumpy rabbit.